MW01250727

Deeply in the Soul

Hristina Bloomfield

Deeply in the Soul

Copyright © 2022 Hristina Bloomfield

All rights reserved.

London, 2022

hrisisart@gmail.com

All characters in this book are fictional, and any resemblance to persons living or dead is purely coincidental.

1

THE WORLD TURNED UPSIDE DOWN

As always, she got up early, put on her old sports gear and headed for the stadium. The air was cool with a hint of drizzle. The stadium was empty. Xena began the first lap slowly. Running calmed her and gave her energy for the rest of the day. In the early quiet, she could hear her every step. She avoided looking down at her feet in fear of seeing her old sneakers falling apart. A few more night shifts at the club and she would probably be able to buy a new pair of trainers. Xena picked up the pace, took a deep breath of fresh air and looked around slowly. The stadium was in a wooded area surrounded on one side by a pine forest. On the other side were deciduous trees, mostly walnuts and chestnuts. A light mist drifted as the night rain evaporated. Not even birds could be heard this morning. Just silence.

Xena usually spent half an hour alone with nature, and that was the best part of her morning. She loved spring mornings. She also loved autumn when the leaves from the trees changed colour and the mountain became pleasantly colourful. Xena ran slowly, devoted to her thoughts, and did not feel the passage of time. She just counted *one, two, three, four* and again *one, two, three, four*.

This helped her concentrate on running. She knew some people hummed a tune as they ran and that helped them with the pace but counting helped her to run evenly and breathe properly. After a few more laps, Xena began to feel the gaze of others. People had woken up. There were always observers, even if she didn't see them, she knew they were there. She could feel their gaze as she turned her back on them, a small tickle in her neck that told her that someone was watching her closely.

By the end of her run the nearby cafe was filled with local people, drinking their morning coffee together and discussing the latest news and gossip. She knew each of them. The town was small, and everyone knew everyone.

Xena was at the end of her run. She started the last lap at a brisk pace and then ran the last two hundred metres at a fast sprint. By the end, she was sweaty and tired. She walked slowly home after waving goodbye to everyone in the cafe. They waved back.

After running, Xena usually went home and slept for another two or three hours. She had become accustomed to running early but she worked late so needed a short nap. In the afternoons she sometimes worked in the shop. Although she worked two jobs, the pay was low, and she could barely pay her bills. She had lived alone for the last five years since the death of her grandmother. Her grandmother had raised her when her mother had abandoned her, and her father never wanted to see her. After her grandmother died, Xena was left alone. She only had her job and her friends.

In the evenings she would spend time with Ivan. They had known each other since childhood. They were neighbours, and at some point, their relationship had deepened. Ivan was two years older than her, and he had protected her since she was a child. She couldn't imagine her life without him. Xena thought of Ivan now. He was tall with dark brown hair that lightened in the summer. His eyes were dark brown, almost black and when he narrowed them, the irises almost disappeared into the blackness of his pupils. Ivan had invited Xena to a date when she was fourteen years old. They met at the same stadium where she ran almost every morning. There he had kissed her for the very first time.

She liked to remember that time and talk to Ivan about it. He often told her that they were just kids back then. Xena remembered the first time he had told her that he loved her. This happened during one of their walks in the mountains. They had climbed to the top and sat on one of the rocks, watching the town from above. The view from the peak had been stunning, and Xena had promised to go there again one day. There, as she had looked at the beautiful landscape around them, he had watched her with an obvious adoration, and then he told her. It had been romantic. Xena thought of how inseparable the two of them had been.

Unfortunately, as time went on, they had spent less and less time together. Especially lately, she had hardly seen him. He sometimes came to see her at the nightclub but there they could not exchange a word. Like her he worked in two places and was seldom free.

Just as she was thinking of him, he called her and asked her to meet him. This surprised her because they usually met at their friends' houses or at her house later.

After her nap and her shift at the store, Xena changed her clothes and left for the meeting. She left early because she hated being late. On the way she stopped to talk to few people.

 The weather had worsened, and the rain had intensified but she decided not to return for an umbrella. She walked slowly as the rain ran down her face. Her clothes were getting wet. Rainwater flowed down the road and her trainers filled with it, making her walk more slowly. Xena ignored the rain. She had grown accustomed to the rain, living here. She looked into the distance at the hills which were shrouded in mist. The mountain was quiet, the air fresh. Rivulets of water ran between the trees, gathering into a small stream along the path. Sometimes the water would detect a rock and go around it with a slight curve meandering its way down to the river. All the small streams flowed into it. The river was calm, not yet stirred by the heavy rain. Here and there she could see barbels and other small river fish swimming downstream. Xena's gaze settled on two figures on the other side of the river. She was almost there.

When she arrived, she saw Ivan talking to Long One. Long One was like the owner of the town. Everything happened only with his permission. Only his men worked in the municipality and the police. He was known as a dangerous man and most people were afraid of him. Xena had served him drinks at the nightclub, but she avoided talking with him. She didn't know what Ivan had to do with Long One. She had a bad feeling. She thought for a moment that it was better not to meet them, but then they saw her, and it was too late to escape.

Ivan motioned for her to approach. His face was flushed, his body betraying fear and some other strong emotion. Xena approached them slowly. Her intuition told her something was wrong. Long One stood a step away from Ivan. When Xena approached, he motioned for her to stand beside him. However, she kept her distance waiting for Ivan to say something. The tension between the two men could be felt even from a distance. When she looked more closely, she saw with horror that Ivan's mouth was bleeding. His T-shirt had absorbed some of the blood, mixing with the rain. Xena guessed that their argument had lasted a long time because they both looked tired and visibly cold.

Xena shivered. In this area the river made a turn and entered the forest slightly which made the place very cold. The sun rarely managed to warm this spot. The two men stood facing each other. Both with pursed lips. Long One stared at Ivan and told him to speak. Ivan, however, remained silent.

'Tell her!' Long One shouted. Ivan continued not to speak. His gaze was fixed on his shoes.

'Tell her!'

This time Long One grabbed Ivan by the elbow and made him moan. Xena was in shock and waited for what he might say. The rain was still pouring, chilling her to the bone. She bit her lip in tension. She was waiting for Ivan to say something. His hands trembled and he put them in his pockets. He wouldn't look at her, and her sense of doom intensified. Xena didn't make it easy, didn't ask a question and kept waiting in silence.

'Xena, I...' Ivan began but it was hard for him to continue. His gaze was still down.

'Tell her,' Long One shouted angrily.

'He already owns you,' Ivan barely whispered.

Xena stared in bewilderment. How did Long One own her? She knew from the other girls that if you owed him a lot, he would force you into prostitution. She didn't owe him anything, she only served him drinks, and in her confusion, she wondered whether Ivan had a debt with him, but she thought that Ivan wasn't a gambler.

'Tell her why,' Long One ordered.

Ivan still looked down.

'I failed to return his money on time, and you were the bet.'

Xena froze. She and Ivan were very close, if he needed money, he would've told her. She didn't understand what was going on.

'You didn't tell me you were short on money,' she said, speaking for the first time. Her voice was even, there was no emotion in it, but her mouth was trembling and that betrayed her fear.

'But he told me. I gave him a few thousand, but it was hard for him to pay it off. He offered you in return. You against his life. You know how I work. I don't forgive debtors.' Long One's gaze circled her body.

Xena frowned at the sight. She continued to watch Ivan. She expected an explanation, but he did not speak. He studied the water.

'What was the money for?' she asked.

Ivan didn't answer and that infuriated her.

'What did you need that money for?' she shouted.

He still didn't answer.

'It won't happen. I won't pay your debts. Either tell me now, or I'm leaving.' Xena flinched as Long One grabbed her with one leap and pulled her close.

'No, sweetie, you're not leaving. You stay with me and from now on you will do what I tell you.'

Xena froze, then tried to free herself, but Long One was strong and tough. He had caught her with a quick grip, apparently accustomed to such quarrels. She looked at her boyfriend again. He was silent, looking away from her.

'You don't own me,' she told Long One. 'I don't owe you anything. Let me go.'

She knew there was no point in shouting. There was only one house here near this part of the river and it was owned by Long One. No one would help her. Xena panicked. She was unprepared for such a thing. Ivan's silence drove her crazy. What had he done, why was he silent and why didn't he tell her anything? Whatever it was, she would have understood and helped him. However, he did not move. The only sound coming from him was sniffing.

Long One's phone rang, he reached out to get it out of his pocket and Xena took advantage of the distraction. She hit him hard with her elbow in the abdomen and started running stepping into the river. She could hear the footsteps of the approaching man and Ivan's screams.

'Don't leave me, Xena! He will kill me if you don't do what he wants. Xena, stop! Please!'

But she didn't stop. Then she felt the breath of Long One beside her. He grabbed her leg and knocked her down.

'There's nowhere to run,' he said, grinning.

Xena crashed into the river which was becoming more violent. She felt something wooden, grabbed it tightly and struck Long One on his chest with as much force as she could. He swayed but did not fall. He pulled the rod from her hand and aimed it at her abdomen. Once and then once more, he ended up with a blow aimed at her head, but she turned at the last moment and the rod hit her shoulder. The pain stunned her.

At that moment she saw the water dragging Long One. He had lost his balance as he turned to hit her. Xena took a deep breath and dived into the deep part of the river. She swam downstream for a few minutes, turned briefly and when she couldn't see anyone, she hurried out of the water and slipped into the woods. Xena was shaking. She tried not to run, though she instinctively wanted to. Running would scare the birds and that would quickly reveal her location.

She walked slowly and carefully. She could hear her own footsteps and though she tried to be as quiet as possible the needles of the pine trees on the ground made a soft noise. The sun was going down. Soon, the mountain would be completely dark, and with the darkness would come the cold.

Xena moved slowly, the branches of the bushes and trees hitting her and sometimes she fell to the ground, but she got up quickly. Her fear forced her on. She had read somewhere that it didn't matter how many times you fell, it was important to be able to get up after each fall, and now, subconsciously, she was doing just that. Regardless of the physical and emotional pain, she had to go on and go where...

The thought shocked her. She had nowhere to go. Long One would look for her in her house and in the house of her friends. There was no way she could go to Ivan's house anymore. He had sold her for a few thousands. She had heard of such fates, but she had never expected it to be hers. She would think about it later. Now she needed dry clothes and a place where no one would look for her.

Xena loved the mountains but only during the day. At night the mountains frightened her. The landscape became unfamiliar, dark, and gloomy. She felt the moisture around her gather. The noises of the nocturnal animals frightened her. The cold clung to her skin, and she could feel it in every bone. Her clothes were soaked with water, and pine needles and dry leaves were clinging to them. The cold frightened her and so did the fear. She began to run on the spot to keep warm or perhaps to get rid of the feeling of helplessness.

Where should I go now? she wondered.

She stopped, then climbed a high cliff and saw the lights of the town. It was warm there, Xena thought, and the very thought warmed her a little. She looked around the village and wondered where Long One wouldn't look for her. One way or another, he owned everyone in this town. No one would help her for fear of getting into trouble. She needed an uninhabited house. Somewhere with warm blankets and clothes and to be away from the town centre. Then she remembered Granny Dora's house. The old woman died two weeks ago. Her daughter had visited for the funeral and then returned to her family in Sofia. The house was empty. Dora and her daughter were not close. The young woman had moved to Sofia a few years ago and didn't like returning to her mother's.

Dora and Xena's grandmother were close friends, so Xena knew the house very well. Dora took care of her like a nanny when she was little. No one would look for her in the abandoned house. People in the town were superstitious and believed that a deceased soul lived in the house for forty days after death. She knew that Long One was superstitious, too. He would not search that house. Especially at night.

All that remained was the question of how to enter it without the neighbours seeing her. Xena had to wait at least until midnight then sneak past the two houses next door. Until then she would run on the spot to stir her blood. Her hands trembled and her stomach ached. Long One's blows were strong when he hit her in the river, he must have hurt something, but she didn't want to think about it now.

Water was still flowing from the trees. The rain had stopped but with each movement of the branches drops of rainwater were scattering on her. Her clothes and hair would not dry quickly. Xena tried to ignore the noise around her. There were no predators in this mountain, only bears but they did not go down to the village.

After running for a little while longer, she climbed the rock again and watched the sleeping town. Little by little the lights went out. It was dark everywhere on the side of Dora's house. Xena figured it would take her about an hour to get there so it was time to go. She would have to sneak in unnoticed, and she hoped that the spare key to the house was still in its place.

Xena began to descend slowly between the trees. From time to time, she stopped and tried to orient herself, not wanting to lose her way and find herself in the wrong part of the town. She was convinced that Long One's men were still looking for her. She had to avoid entering the streets and being seen under the streetlamps.

Fortunately, Dora's house was one of the last in the upper part of the town, far from the centre.

She was progressing slowly, but she was convinced she was going in the right direction. But there was another obstacle that had to be crossed—the river. Now the river was turbulent, and Xena had to find a place to cross where the current was weaker. She couldn't risk being seen on the bridges. She was glad she had been able to sleep during the day, if she hadn't slept now, she wouldn't have had the strength to cross the river.

Xena stood on the shore and tried to figure out where it was safer to cross. She could hear the river, and feel it, but all she could see were reflections of the light flickering from the rebounds. She couldn't figure out where it was safe and decided to take a risk and move from where she stood. She thought she would be very lucky if she could cross to the other side.

Xena began to wade into the water and tried to keep her balance. It was clear to her that at some point she would have to swim but she wanted to postpone that moment for as long as possible. Xena walked slowly. She stepped carefully until she reached a strong current then took a deep breath and began to swim. It took her a few minutes to reach the other side. Whistling and trembling, she sat near two covenant bushes. After a few seconds, she got up and began to walk quickly. Xena went out on the road near the river and looked around carefully. There were no passing cars. She heard no other noises. She held her breath to make sure she didn't miss any sounds and crossed the road slowly.

Dora's house was not far away. It took her ten minutes to reach it. She began to move more slowly as she approached the town, not wanting to attract any attention. Then she waited opposite the house, checking no one was around.

The neighbourhood was in silence and darkness. Xena approached Dora's house, looked around, and hurried into the garden. She moved one of the pots and picked up the spare key. It was the same, slightly rusty, with an old rubber band that served as a keychain. She tried to unlock the door silently, but the old door made a scraping sound. The hinges were old and noisy. Xena had no choice, she had to take a risk and get inside quickly, hoping no one would hear the creaking of the opening. Xena hoped the neighbours were fast asleep. She slipped inside quickly and entered the house.

After closing the door Xena relaxed and sat in the hallway for a moment. She listened again, wanting to make sure no one saw her then got up, went into the kitchen, and looked out the window at the street. There were no streetlamps on this road, but most people had installed lamps in front of their front doors. Not seeing anyone Xena went upstairs and wrapped herself in a blanket. Her body was still shaking. She really wanted to make herself a cup of tea, but she knew it was dangerous to turn on any appliances. She looked around in the twilight, urgently needing to change her clothes and opened the closet and chose a shirt and a long skirt. Dora had never worn trousers, so Xena wasn't wasting her time looking for something more comfortable. She changed quickly and wrapped herself in two blankets. Then began to massage her body slowly; this would help her blood circulation. Her hair was still wet, and she tried to dry it using the edges of the blanket. The house was old and cold, but still preferable to the rain outside.

Xena sat on the old sofa in the living room and tried to calm down and think. Her head ached badly, and her belly throbbed where Long One had hit her with the wooden stick. She had to find something to stop the pain. Dora had a small first aid kit in the kitchen. Xena hoped there was still medicine in it. She got up slowly, walked to the kitchen, but didn't get far. Her stomach tightened, she felt dizzy and was forced to sit on the floor. The tension of the last few hours began to affect her; her whole body hurt. After a few minutes, Xena made another attempt to get up, reached the kitchen and sat down to rest again. The third time she managed to reach the first aid kit. She calmed down when she saw the painkillers inside and with one last effort went to the tap and took two pills. Xena hoped they would work soon.

A few minutes later her headache subsided. She could think more clearly. The pain in her stomach continued, but Xena tried not to think about it. She had to find a way to leave the town. She didn't have much money, only a twenty, which she wore in her bra for emergencies. Without money she would not get far. The pain returned and Xena decided to take another pill. A few minutes later, warmed by the blankets and relaxed by the painkillers, Xena fell asleep.

She awoke two hours later to a noise in front of the house. Someone was talking. She tried to remember if she had locked the door after entering, but that moment was lost. She held her breath and waited.

'She's not likely to be here.'

The voice was male, Xena didn't recognise it.

'I don't think that someone would come to this house. The old woman's spirit is still here,' the man continued to speak.

Someone approached the door and pressed the handle. The door was locked. She had locked it herself.

'It's locked.' This time the voice belonged to Long One 'But look here, there are wet marks. They may be from her.'

'It could be a cat or a dog,' the stranger said.

'Maybe. Still, I want to check. Tomorrow we will come back and open the door. The bitch is hardly inside, but I don't want to leave things unchecked. Come on, we'll check on her friend again.'

The two men walked away. Xena realised that she could only stay two or three more hours in the house. She had to move as fast as possible.

The friend they were checking on was Adelina. Everyone called her Adi or the Blonde Adi, as the men called her among themselves. Adi was beautiful, and always smiling. When Xena was little, the other children's parents forbade their children to play with her. Without a mother and a father, Xena was not good enough for them. Adi's parents were no exception, but Adi stubbornly disregarded this from an early age. She was the only child who bothered to talk to Xena and her grandmother. Then Ivan showed up and they were all Xena's friends. Years later, her classmates tried to get closer to her, but she never managed to get rid of the feeling that she was not wanted. Her trust was not easy to gain, but it was quick to lose. She was used to being considered special and lonely. Of course, as a bartender and waiter she had to talk to people, but the nightclub conversations were never personal, at least not for her.

The only people who knew her fears and dreams were Ivan and Adi. Ivan was not part of her life now. She wondered if Long

One would really kill him. Many people liked Ivan, he was popular in the town and if people found out that Long One had taken his life, it would not have a good effect on his reputation. He was cruel in many other ways, but at least Xena didn't think he had killed anyone before, not physically. Long One was good at psychological harassment. He knew how to get people to work for him and often hurt them physically, as a lesson to others, to be aware that he was not joking. He never cut fingers, hands, or feet. He made visible physical scars, but he didn't kill. Or at least she hadn't heard of it ever happening. In the situation she was in, she was in greater danger than Ivan. No one ran away from Long One. Everyone paid off their debt in one way or another. But this debt wasn't hers.

Xena wondered again why Ivan needed money and why he hadn't told her. And why he had betrayed her in this way. He hadn't trusted her, and that drove her crazy. They were very close, like brother and sister. They were also lovers. But how close could two people really be, she wondered.

Severe pain brought her back to reality. It had been several hours since she had taken the last painkiller and it was time for another one. Xena took two pills and sat down at the table. She needed a plan. Dawn was beginning outside. There was not much time and there weren't many options. The only way to leave town was by bus. She didn't have a driver's license, she couldn't steal a car, and going back to the woods wasn't a good option. All that left was the bus.

The first bus to Sofia was in about an hour. Probably someone would be watching the passengers, so she had to disguise herself. The other problem was money. The money she had would not be enough for a ticket.

Xena looked around, wondering if Dora had left any of her money in the attic. When she was little, Xena had gone up there once secretly. She had searched for treasures and, to her surprise, found one. Dora had saved some money and hidden it in a small box. When Xena grew up and Dora's health deteriorated, the old woman herself told her about the money. She trusted her. Xena, however, did not know if Dora's daughter knew about this box. Maybe she had taken it when she came for the funeral. She had to check.

Xena looked for a chair, tried to ignore the pain in her stomach and stepped on the chair. The ladder was in the garden, there was no way to use it. She had to find strength and go up to the attic. On her second attempt she succeeded. The attic was dirty and dark. It was as if no one had gone up there in years. Xena leaned forward and groped for the small box. She sneezed but managed to dull the sound with her palms. There was dust everywhere. The attic reawakened memories of her childhood, but she quickly turned her attention to the money. She had to find it if it was still there. The box was not where she had found it as a child. It looked like the daughter had taken it after all. Xena walked around the attic just in case and finally saw it. The box was smaller than she remembered, but it was definitely there. She recognised the little rose that adorned it. Now she saw that the box had contained soap before it became a piggy bank. She opened it and a smile lit up her face. The money was inside. There was enough to escape the town. She took the notes and slowly came down from the attic, trying not to make any noise in case the neighbours woke up.

Satisfied with what she found, Xena went to the bedroom, reopened the closet, and examined the clothes inside. She had to disguise herself. Dora was one of the village's artists. Xena was not interested in theatre, she did not want to become an actor and did not pay much attention to what the old woman showed her, but one day she had seen Dora looking at least twenty years older and had been startled. Then she had asked Dora to show her how to apply makeup, what to emphasise and where. Xena once managed to scare Adi with her appearance after she put on makeup.

Now she had to take advantage of this knowledge and change her age beyond recognition. She picked up the makeup bag and went to the bathroom. The room had no windows and she turned on the light. Her plan was to put on Dora's clothes, and to put on a big hat and makeup so that no one would recognise her. The makeup took about twenty minutes. It was half an hour before the bus was due to leave. She had to go to the bus station at the last minute so as not to give people much time to look at her. It was also important to know who would be on the bus. She had to make sure no one spoke to her.

Xena wore a blouse, a knitted vest, and a long skirt. Dora's shoes were two sizes smaller, and her feet would hurt but she would last. Either way she would have to take painkillers, they would dull the pain. She lifted her hair into a bun and put on a hat. Xena looked in the mirror and even she couldn't recognise herself. She writhed in pain again. This gave her an even older look. She looked at her watch again and wished herself success.

Xena quietly unlocked the door and hurried out of the house. She turned quickly around the corner, then leaned forward and walked slowly toward the bus station. She tried to walk slightly hunched over and the pain in her stomach was helping. At six-twenty-five she stood in front of the bus door and waited her turn for a ticket. There were four people in front of her. One of them motioned for her to pass in front of him. He obviously considered her as old and weak. As she climbed the step, someone grabbed her elbow and forced her to turn. He was one of Long One's men. He looked at her from head to toe and apologised. Xena bought a ticket with her hands trembling with fear and moved slowly inside the bus. She found a place out of sight and sat down, putting her hat on to cover herself from most of the passengers. She pulled a small plastic bottle from the handbag she had taken from Dora's house and took two pills.

Xena couldn't wait for the bus to leave. Long One's man continued to check the passengers and paid no more attention to her. She thought that Dora continued to help her even after her death. One of the few people who did not disappoint her. The sad thing was that she couldn't say goodbye to one of her loved ones, her best friend must have been worried about her. She missed Adi already. She even missed Ivan, but not the Ivan she last saw.

Finally, the bus left. Xena sighed with relief and rested her head on the backrest. She could now afford a short break. In three hours, they were to arrive in Sofia. Until then, she would be asleep.

2

OLD END, NEW BEGINNING

Xena woke up with severe abdominal pain. At first, she didn't know where she was, then she felt the rumble of the bus and saw the passengers and remembered. She looked out of the window. The first blocks of the big city could be seen in the distance. Xena had come to Sofia a few times on various occasions. She didn't know the city well, but that didn't bother her. The important thing was to be away from Long One. Xena pressed her hand to her stomach and tried to ignore the pain. Her head hurt too, she felt like her blood was flowing. She would deal with that when she arrived.

Her thoughts returned to Ivan. Her soul ached when she thought of him. He had sold her. She couldn't believe that someone would do such a thing to someone they loved. "You were the bet." His words stuck in her head. Why would he pledge a human being against a loan? Aren't houses, properties, things without a soul and feelings a better stake? Her eyes began to water. Two kinds of pain were cutting her into small pieces at the moment: the physical pain and the pain of the wounded soul. She felt alone and abandoned. That feeling she had felt as a child when she realised that her parents had abandoned her. It returned with double force. Xena sobbed. A man in the seat next to her asked if she was okay. She replied that she was fine, but she really wasn't. The man's voice brought her back to reality and she looked out the window. The coach station was already visible, gloomy, and as dark as the weather. It was raining and as the builders worked and dug around it was muddy.

The bus stopped slowly, and the passengers began to disembark. Xena decided to come down last. She waited for everyone, picked up Dora's handbag and walked slowly across the bus. The handbag was her only luggage. She had no clothes and no personal belongings. Fortunately, she had an ID if she ever had to use it. She hoped no one would ask questions.

The first thing she wanted to buy were clothes. No one would rent her a room if they saw her in her current state.

After leaving the coach station, Xena crossed a few blocks and headed for a street she knew had shops. She saw a second-hand clothing store and went there, but at that moment a severe pain in her groin forced her to squat. She couldn't breathe through the pain. She felt the blood run down her face. Her eyes blurred. Xena instinctively pulled the handbag toward her and curled into a ball.

'Are you okay?' she heard a female voice ask, but she could not answer. Xena lost consciousness and collapsed on the sidewalk.

Xena woke up to the sound of voices. Someone was talking near her. She tried to open her eyes, but her eyelids were too heavy. She took a deep breath and sighed. It smelled like a hospital. She remembered fainting and she wondered where she was. Her head was heavy, and she couldn't think very well. Xena fell asleep again. It was dark when she woke up again. She could hear breathing on both sides. She struggled to her feet and saw that she was in a hospital room. There were five more beds in the room. Four of them were occupied, one was empty. She remembered the seizure and wondered how long she had been here. Xena removed the blanket and saw that she was wearing a white cotton nightgown printed with small blue flowers. She lifted her nightgown slowly and her gaze fell on a bandage on her abdomen. Instead of her panties she was wearing an adult's nappy. Xena tried to get up, but her legs were too weak and there was pain in her groin. Apparently, the blows Long One had inflicted on her had torn something inside her. She felt peak and weak again. She settled on the bed, rested her head, and fell asleep again.

Xena hoped to be able to walk in the morning. She instinctively knew that she was not safe in the hospital. If her name had been written down somewhere, Long One would have found her. He had people everywhere and he knew she was injured. He would look for her till the last. Xena fell asleep, but this time her sleep was restless. She dreamed of muddy water, shouts, and blows.

'Are you okay?' Xena heard a familiar voice. The woman who asked her was the same one who asked her this question before she collapsed on the sidewalk.

Xena opened her eyes and saw a friendly young woman. Her eyes were worried, but there was something beautiful about her. Xena couldn't tell what it was, but it certainly reassured her.

'I'm fine thanks. Where am I?'

'In the Accident and Emergency room. You've been here for three days.'

'Three days?' Xena asked. There was fear in her voice.

'Don't worry,' the woman said. 'Nobody knows you're here. I saw the clothes and the makeup. No one pretends to be so old and ugly for no reason.'

Xena rested her head on the pillow with relief. This woman had already saved her life once, now maybe twice.

'What is your name?' Xena asked her.

'Darina, but everyone calls me Dary.'

Xena looked at the young woman without hiding her gaze. Dary had light brown hair, her eyes were light, a mixture of pale blue, grey and green. Her nose was slightly upturned, giving her a girlish look. Everything in this woman breathed freshness and her gaze was undisguised. Xena liked her right away, she somehow managed to gain her trust and that wasn't typical for her. It usually took her years to trust someone.

'Thanks, Dary. For everything.' Then Xena timidly asked, 'My bag?'

'It's in my locker. I'll give it to you when you're discharged. I kept everything as it is.'

'Thank you,' Xena said again. 'You shouldn't have had to worry so much.'

'Your old clothes are soaked in blood. There is no way to leave with them. What do you want me to do with them?'

'Throw them away, please.'

'All right.' Dary looked at Xena sadly and said, 'I'm sorry about the baby.'

'The baby?' Xena wondered. 'What baby?'

Dary sighed.

'You didn't know you were pregnant?'

'No,' Xena said softly. Her mouth went dry. Her emotions knocked her back on the pillow and she wept softly. No, she didn't know she was pregnant. She hadn't even thought about it. Ivan and she didn't want children. They had no money to look after themselves, they could not take care of another human being. Xena closed her eyes and her tears flowed. Big sad tears. She could feel the eyes of the other women in the room.

'I'm sorry for your loss, child!' an older woman said. 'There's nothing worse than losing your child.'

The old lady approached Xena's bed and began stroking her hair. This caused even more tears. This time she did not hide that she was crying. She indulged in her pain. In just a few days, she lost almost everyone in her life and now her child, of whom she didn't even know. Xena no longer wanted to live. She didn't want to fight. She only wanted to forget and die if she could.

'Here, take this,' Dary said, handing her a pill and a plastic cup of water. 'It will help you calm down.'

Xena reached for the pill, her hand trembling. She tried to take the glass of water, but her tremor intensified, and she spilled some of the water. Sobbing and with trembling lips, she tried to stop the trembling and finally took the pill. It didn't work immediately. Tears streamed down her skin long before she calmed down and fell asleep.

Dary woke her.

'Zornitsa, you have to get up and eat.'

Xena struggled to her feet and looked into the young woman's eyes.

'Please call me Xena.'

'All right, Xena. Can you get up?'

Xena got up slowly, managing to get to her feet. Dary supported her and helped her into the dining room.

'You have to eat to recover. You will have to start getting up and walking to get stronger again.'

'How much longer do I have to stay here?'

'Three days, if your recovery is going well. I won't let you go until I see you're well.'

The dining room was half-full. Few people looked at her, but most ate staring at the plates in front of them. The smell of food restored her appetite. Xena slowly joined the people as she waited for food. She took the portion, but her hands trembled. A sullen young man helped her and carried the tray of food to one of the nearby tables.

'Thank you,' Xena said softly. He nodded and returned to his food.

As she ate, Xena surveyed the people around her. She had never had to be in the hospital before. As a child, she often went to the A&E department because she always was accident-prone. She remembered her childhood, wandering in the mountains with Ivan and their friends. They always came back with a scratch or two, but this was different. The smell of disinfectant suffocated her. Also, the obvious pain that some of the people around her were feeling. What was it like to work here, among sick people and souls? Xena knew one thing; it wasn't for her. As a bartender she had to listen to people's stories and their pain. People rarely shared anything joyful or positive with the bartender. Talking to them for a while was no problem for her, but it was different here at the hospital. Here she felt vulnerable, weak and she didn't like it, she couldn't stay surrounded by sick people for long. It would depress her.

A few minutes later, Dary returned to help her return to her room.

'How are you doing here, among all these patients?' Xena asked her.

'I am used to it. My father was a doctor. You could say I grew up in a hospital.'

'It is very depressing for me.'

'It's normal for you to feel like that. Most people don't like being here.'

'What do I have to do to get out of here? Do I have to sign any documents?' Xena asked.

'No, you can leave when you're ready. However, I think you should stay at least another day. Is there a place for you to go? Do you want to call someone to pick you up? I saw you don't have a phone. You can use mine if you want.'

'I have no one to call,' Xena whispered softly. Her voice trembled slightly. 'But I'll find a place to stay.'

'I know this might seem strange, but I have a suggestion,' Dary said. 'You can stay with me temporarily. My roommate left for two months. Her room is empty, and the rent is paid.'

'Dary, thank you for everything you have done for me, but I don't want to interfere you with my mess. You could get hurt because of me.'

'Why? What happened to you? Who are you running from?'

'The less you know, the better. I don't want to sound ungrateful, but the truth is, I don't want to cause you any trouble.'

'Okay, it is your decision. Tell me if you change your mind.'

They talked quietly so that the other patients in the room could not hear them.

Dary leaned over and whispered softly in Xena's ear, 'I'll get you some clothes and a pair of trainers tomorrow. The ones you came with were soaked in blood and I threw them away.'

'Thanks. I'll give you money for the new ones before I leave. I promise!'

'You won't have to. They will not be new, just washed. One of our roommates left a large piece of luggage two years ago. She left for Britain and never returned. You look a lot like her, both in physique and face. At first, I thought you were her. That is one of the reasons why I helped you.'

'All right,' Xena said. 'I'm really grateful to you. I just don't want to get you in trouble.'

'See you tomorrow,' Dary said. 'Be sure to go to dinner, if you can go around the room and the hallways. It will help you get stronger.'

'I'll do it,' Xena said. She wished she could run to the stadium again in the morning. To feel the coolness of the mountain, the song of the birds and the beauty of the sunrise. She missed everything right now. Even Ivan. What was happening to him now? How would he pay off his debt? And if she had known earlier that she was pregnant, would it have been different? What had he gotten himself into? Xena couldn't even imagine that much money. Her monthly salary barely exceeded a hundred. A thousand seemed like a cosmic sum to her and a few thousand didn't even seem possible. What did Ivan do with that money? And most importantly, why hadn't he told her? The truth was that for several months they had hardly seen each other and when that happened, they focused mainly on sex. They hardly talked. Xena didn't worry about that, in most cases she and Ivan got along without words, but now that she was mentally going back, she could feel the distance and his desire to leave faster. She had even thought of asking him if there was a problem, but everyday life kicked her, and she never did. What shocked her the most was that he used her as a bet. Her body, her soul. How could a person love someone and do such a thing?

Did he really love her? This question had bothered her since she woke up in the hospital. Her closest person, a person with whom she spent most of her life, for whom she would otherwise sacrifice and for whom she would die for. He sold her. He had begged her to agree to be sold without even explaining why. These thoughts caused a new stream of tears. Xena curled up in bed, turned her back on the room and cried. Quiet at first, then she couldn't stop sobbing. Facing the wall, all she saw were smudged stains. Her eyes were watery with tears. Xena felt her pulse and temperature rise. She tried to calm down, though she knew it was better to cry. Thousands of tears would not stop the emotion she felt, the sadness, the sorrow, and the helplessness. This vulnerability she felt when she was a child. The crying exhausted her, and she finally fell asleep. A deep, healthy sleep.

She woke up for dinner. This time she managed to go to the dining room on her own. Her hands were still trembling, so the sullen young man helped her carry the food to the table again. Xena thanked him with a slight smile. She ate, went back to bed, and began to think about what she would do next. She needed to contact Adi.

Her friend must have been worried about her. They had always had a way to share secret messages. Adi's mother hadn't wanted her to mess with Xena, and so that she wouldn't find out they were still friends, Xena and Adi made a cipher. Xena decided to take advantage of Dary's offer to use her phone. She would write a message to Adi, telling her she was fine and not to worry about her. So deep in thought for her friend, Xena fell asleep again. Dary woke her in the morning. She had brought her clothes and shoes.

'I'll put them in your locker,' she said.

'No. I'll just change and leave. I don't have to stay here anymore. Can I use your phone to send a message?'

'Of course.'

Dary handed her phone and left the room. Xena stared after her. This girl had great confidence in people. She just left her clothes and phone. What if Xena had decided to just leave?

Xena wrote a short message and sent it. She hoped Adi would be happy when she got it. She missed her very much.

Two hours later with Dora's bag in hand, Xena left the hospital. She went outside and looked around. Two things she had to do as quickly as possible: buy a phone, as cheap as possible and find accommodation. Dary forced her to promise that if she didn't find a place to stay tonight, she would go and sleep at hers.

A phone was found quickly, but with the accommodation she had hit a rock. There were no rooms available. She called several agencies and made one viewing only. An elderly woman was renting a room on one of the main streets, but she was only giving the room, she didn't want her bathroom and toilet to be used.

'Then where will I go to the toilet?' Xena asked her.

'Well, outside,' said the old lady. The broker and Xena looked at each other.

Xena wandered the streets until dark, but in the end, it was too late. She was tired and the pain in her abdomen and head intensified. She bought herself a cheap slice of pizza and then called Dary.

'Come home,' said Dary. 'I'll make you a mint tea to keep you warm.'

An hour later, Xena was drinking tea in Dary's kitchen.

'Thanks! I don't know what I would do without you. I would have probably gone to a mall until they closed and then I don't know.'

'Don't worry and don't apologise. I've been in your situation, and I know how difficult it is.'

'You said your father is a doctor. Where is he now?'

'He died many years ago. My mother too. Two years ago, my uncle sold the house we lived in, and I found myself alone on the street. Before you ask, the house belonged to Grandma and my uncle was the heir. He is my only relative. I haven't seen him since and I don't want to see him. That's how I got here. My mother left me some money. I invested in education and so I became a nurse. I wanted to work as a doctor, as my father did, but I can't afford the high fees at university. And you? What happened to you?'

'Let's just say I got involved in something I had no idea about and had to run. It is better for you not to know the details.'

'Can you return to your hometown? Do you have relatives?'

'I can't go back, at least for now. My only relative is my childhood friend.'

'I'm sorry and I understand,' Dary whispered.

'Dary, it is very important that if someone asks you about me not to tell him anything. To say you don't know me. Promise me,' Xena's voice trembled and so did her hand. She forced herself to leave the cup of tea on the table so as not to spill it. She wouldn't forgive herself if something happened to Dary.

'I won't tell anyone. I promise. You can stay here until you find accommodation.'

'Thank you,' Xena said wearily.

Xena slept until late in the morning. She made herself a coffee, did some exercise and started looking for a place to live again. She couldn't arrange a tour until noon, so she decided to look for a job. Xena still had Dora's money, but she preferred not to spend it. It was borrowed, she would put it back in the attic box one day. She browsed ads for bartenders and waiters. There were only two ads. She knew that finding a job was the difficult thing. As it turned out, it was not easy to find accommodation either.

To Xena's surprise, they were still looking for a worker in the second place. The cafe was small, with five tables. The owner, a large woman with a lot of makeup on her face, looked at her from head to toe and grumbled.

'Let's see what you can do.'

She made Xena make her some coffee and pour her a few cups of soft drinks. She talked all the time, telling Xena about her personal life and her problems with her boyfriend, who had a mistress. In about an hour, Xena knew the owner's entire love life. Her name was Svetla. Xena let her talk and complain. She served a few customers, wiped the bar, and looked into the kitchen. Sandwiches were made in the cafe and from what she knew, if she accepted the job, she had to do everything herself. About an hour later, Svetla offered Xena the job. The pay was twice as good as in her hometown and she accepted.

She would have to work six days a week from 9 a.m. to 8 p.m. Xena hadn't expected to find a job so quickly and the fact that there were no other candidates for the job had surprised her. There was something strange about it, but she didn't have many options. She would leave if something turned out to be really wrong.

Xena decided to explore this place more tomorrow.

She returned to Dary's house and began cooking. At least she could make dinner as a thank you. A few hours later Dary returned. As soon as she came home, Xena had felt something bothering her.

'I made potato stew for dinner. I hope you like it.'

'Thank you,' Dary said with a slight smile. 'I received a very strange message today. I think it is a response to what you sent.'

Dary handed the phone to Xena. She looked at the message and froze.

'I didn't kill him,' she said. 'I don't know why Adi thinks that.'

'Look, Xena, I feel like you are good person, but your friend claims you killed someone named Ivan. I don't want anything to do with a killer.'

'I didn't kill him. I didn't even know he was dead'.

Tears welled up in Xena's eyes. They ran down her cheeks and dripped on to her T-shirt. She sobbed loudly and went into her room. She curled up on the bed and cried without hiding. It was such a shock to find out that Ivan was dead.

'He...' she whispered when she sensed Dary near her, '...he was my best friend. I didn't know he was dead'.

Realising the fact Xena shrank even more. Adi told her that she had been charged with his murder. Her best friend believed that it was not someone else who killed Ivan but her. How was that even possible?

'I'm sorry,' Dary said.

She didn't know what else to say. She didn't know what to do either. Should she call the police and hand her over or give her a chance? Dary needed an explanation.

'Will you tell me what happened? Why were you dressed like an old woman?'

'The last time I saw Ivan he was alive. A man he owed money was stalking me. I had to run away, otherwise I would have belonged to him for life. I swear I didn't kill anyone.'

'Was Ivan the father of your child?' Dary asked.

'Yes,' Xena said softly. Her tears began to flow again. She cried and curled up on the bed again.

Dary went to the kitchen. Xena could hear her moving and turn on the kettle. Would she turn her over to the police? Xena grief quickly turned to fear. These people could find and hurt Dary as well. It was foolish of her to use her phone. She got up quickly and went to the kitchen.

'I made you a peppermint tea to calm you down,' Dary said.

She moved closer to Xena and looked closely at her face. Her grief was sincere, and her tears flowed without stopping, she thought. Even if she were a good actress, it was something she couldn't replay. The young woman's shock was real and Dary wanted to protect her, at least as much as she could. Still, she didn't know what to believe. Her life had taught her not to trust everyone and everything. Dary saw Xena's face freeze at the thought and looked at her questioningly.

'You have to turn off your phone,' Xena said. 'If you don't, they will follow it and find you. I don't want to involve you in this, Dary. Here you are, my phone, if you want to call the police, but please throw out yours right away.'

Dary's face froze, and the shock of Xena's words startled her. She opened the phone and pulled out the SIM card and battery. Then she picked up Xena's phone, pulled it close to her and looked into her eyes.

'I don't know if I should believe you,' she said.

'I can't prove to you that I didn't do anything. I know who killed Ivan, he knows I know and there is another reason to look for me. My very presence here puts you in danger. If you want to call the police, do it now, if you don't, let me go and I'll find a place to sleep.'

'Drink your tea. I won't call the police, not until I'm sure you're guilty. Will you tell me what happened?'

'No. I would prefer not to involve you in this. The less you know, the better.'

'Is your name really Zornitsa?'

'Yes. My ID card is real and if someone is looking for me, they will ask you for that name.'

'All right.' Dary said, leaning back in her chair.

There were dark circles under Dary's eyes. From the moment she saw the message, everything in her had tightened. She didn't know what to do, but her intuition told her not to call the police. Xena already had several opportunities to attack her, but she didn't, which meant she didn't want to hurt her.

Dary got up, poured tea for herself, and sat across from Xena.

'What are you going to do?' she asked.

'I don't know. However, I need to get out of here as soon as possible. Maybe they've already tracked your phone and are coming here to look for me.'

'Where are you going to go?'

'I don't know. I'll look for a hotel for tonight. I will pay more not to have my data recorded.'

'What about tomorrow?' Dary asked. 'You can't sleep there forever.'

'Today I found a job so after work, I'll look for a place to live. Don't worry about me, I'll be fine somehow. I have enough money.'

Dary was silent for a few minutes. She finished her tea and went to the closet in the hallway.

'There are more clothes from my former roommate here. You can take whatever you want, she will hardly come back after so long to look for them.'

'Thank you for your trust,' Xena said.

'I hope I will be not sorry,' Dary said. 'I have one condition. Let me know when you settle down somewhere. I don't want to worry about you.'

'I will.'

Xena went to the closet, checked the contents, and chose a few tops, jeans and two jackets for the season.

She left half an hour later. Dary had also given her a small suitcase for the clothes. It was hard for her to leave her new friend, she already felt very close to her, but she had no choice. Xena walked aimlessly through the streets, thinking how unfair life was. How it gives everything to some and only takes away from others.

Her aimless walk led her to a small motel. She decided to try to sign up under a false name. She filled out the form, wrote the name of an acquaintance of hers from school and a fake ID number. The man at the front desk never asked for her ID. He asked her how many days she would stay. She told him she would stay for a week, then paid and got a temporary motel room.

The atmosphere in the room was depressing, not that she was expecting anything else. The carpet was old, it was torn at the edges, the sheets were in disrepair too, but Xena didn't worry about that. She was grateful to have a roof over her head, to be warm, dry and to have a bed. She didn't need anything else at the moment.

In the morning she bought herself a phone and sent a message to Dary. One smiling face, nothing else. That's how they got along. Every week, she planned to send her a similar message to let Dary know that she was fine.

After sending the message, Xena went and bought a coffee and a newspaper. She did not want to check on the internet for Ivan's murder. She wanted to see if it was in all the media. Xena turned on the TV, read the newspaper and calmed down. There was no mention of such a murder and her name was nowhere to be found. Half an hour later she went to work.

Her boss was already there, lighting a cigarette and drinking a fresh coffee.

'I wasn't sure if you were coming,' she told Xena.

'I accepted the job and now I'm here.'

'Make yourself some coffee and come sit with me,' Svetla told her.

Xena did as she was told.

'I have to tell you something,' Svetla began. 'The work here is a little different from the work in any other cafe.'

Xena said nothing and Svetla continued.

'Rather, the work is the same, but the customers in the cafe are different. They require discretion. Everything you see or hear must remain here. Do you understand?'

Xena nodded. She had been impressed by the clientele yesterday, but she wasn't sure what had bothered her. Now her suspicions were justified, and she could see things more clearly.

'If you tell someone what is happening in the cafe you will affect many interests. You also need to know that we have regular customers. You must learn to recognise them and offer them tables away from the bar. If you start this job today, you will have to comply with these conditions. Should I rely on you or look for someone else?'

'You can count on me,' Xena said.

Svetla looked at her from head to toe.

'Apparently, you're used to not asking questions and keeping secrets,' she said.

'Yes, I'm used to it. That was part of my job with my last employer.'

'What is the name of your last employer?' Svetla asked.

Xena was visibly worried. She shouldn't have said anything about herself. Her face clouded.

'Okay, don't tell me. Obviously, you have secrets too. Now I will let you work. Call me if you have any questions.'

With that, Svetla ended the conversation, got up, finished her coffee at once, and left the cafe. Xena was left alone, and she was angry with herself for talking too much.

A few minutes later, the first customers entered the cafe. It didn't take her long to figure out what her boss was talking about. Most of the customers were police officers and inspectors from the Police Station across the street. The other part were girls and women of different ages. They called themselves companions, but according to Xena, they weren't exactly honest about their profession. Some of the officers were their pimps, others their clients. Xena began to regret accepting the job, but it was too late to give up. This time she had unwittingly plunged into this mess on her own. The strangest thing was that her boss probably thought she accepted her for that.

The work was not difficult, not for Xena. She made about fifty coffees a day and poured just as many soft drinks. Pre-ordered catering came at noon, it was the busiest part of the day, but when lunch was over the cafe was quiet. Most of her clients left good tips. It was the dream job except for the illegal part. Xena tried not to think about it.

Two days later, she managed to find accommodation nearby. In addition to her, two other girls lived in the apartment. Xena liked them but tried to distance herself. She didn't want to answer questions and she stayed longer in her room and studied. After Dary mentioned to her that her former roommate had gone to Britain, Xena started to consider going abroad herself. Somehow, she didn't feel at ease, even in Sofia. Long One could find her here. It would be better if she could go to another country.

For this purpose, she began to study English intensively. She didn't want to take lessons to avoid more meetings and conversations. The fewer people she knew, the less chance Long One had of finding her. The police had not yet signalled to her that she was wanted for a crime.

Xena bought a few English tutorials from the bookstore, downloaded a few videos from the Internet and did just that in her spare time. She memorised words, uttered them and wrote them down.

One day to her surprise, she found Dary's roommate's ID in one of the jackets she had taken from Dary. She looked at the photo and thought Dary was right. They really looked a lot alike. The same blue eyes, the same elongated face, and slightly full lips. The only difference was the colour of her hair. Xena had honey-blonde hair, while the woman in the photo had light brown hair, but it wasn't that different. Besides, some women change the colour of their hair every few months. Xena placed the young woman's ID next to her ID. She could use it in an emergency, although she sincerely hoped she didn't have to. She remembered all the data from it, name, address, and card number. The expiration date was not for two years.

For a few months Xena went to work and studied. She already knew all the customers; they knew her too. Sunday was her day off and the cafe was closed. Her boss came once a week to take over. They rarely talked and if they talk it was only on business. They had accepted this relationship from the beginning and said nothing personal. After a while, Xena realised that nothing Svetla had said on the first day was true. Apparently, all this talking and blabbering on about her boyfriend and his mistress was like a test for the interview. From the female clients, Xena learned that Svetla had a partner, but no one knew who he was. They said they thought he was a high-ranking police officer because the cafe had never been inspected. Neither tax, nor health, nor outhit. People said there was something strange about this whole thing and Xena agreed. She had worked in this business for years and knew about the bribes that the owners of these cafes constantly paid just to get them licenses. She regretted accepting the job. She knew she would have problems if she decided to leave and for now, she was just keeping her fingers crossed that everything would go on as before, without any problems.

Xena found that the customers in the cafe were from three groups. The first group consisted of real customers who came for lunch and coffee from the neighbouring buildings. Most were local, but there were some who worked somewhere nearby. The street was one of the main streets in this area and had several shops and office buildings. The second group consisted of police officers. Some of them ran side businesses and Xena was afraid of them. She often met their gazes, hard, unyielding, and predatory. Two of them eagerly examined her body and even offered her work.

She felt cynical. Life continued to mess with her. How did she get to this place? She hated the second group of customers. They all used their power and the law to make others work for them. To her, these people were on a lower level than even Long One.

The third group of clients were the companions and prostitutes. They were all young, some younger than Xena. They always looked good, always smiling, but when Xena looked deep into their eyes, she saw sadness. Over time, she got to know some of them well. She tried to understand what had happened to them, how they had found themselves in this situation. The strange thing was that each had a different story, but it was all rooted from one thing—love. The girls would meet a handsome and powerful man. They would trust him; they would give themselves to him. Then he started sharing them with his friends and finally controlled them. He started to control their lives, their money, their actions and even their clothes. They continued because they loved this man and wanted to do everything for him. They did not resist. They did it voluntarily. Life was a strange thing. Love was a strange thing.

The stories of these women were like hers, but Xena realised that her love for Ivan was not strong enough to make her go this way. Now he was dead, and she was sad, but her sadness had nothing to do with the sadness in the eyes of these women. She had felt such sadness when her grandmother fell ill, the sadness of doom and helplessness. Sadness for a person you love very much and truly. Xena realised that she had not loved Ivan in this way. She had loved him as a friend. Maybe that's why she ran away and didn't save him. Or maybe he didn't love her deeply and sincerely either. Whatever the reason was, her story was like these women, but not exactly. She sincerely hoped to meet someone who she would love so truly, but she hoped to meet a good man, not the freaks who quietly offered their girlfriends for sale in the cafe.

Usually, there were no clients who were seeking sexual services, but one day two people arrived, and their appearance made Xena bristle. The two men ordered drinks and sat down at the end table. They looked at the women at the bar and paid close attention to Xena. She hid in the kitchen for a while, but she couldn't stay there forever. She went behind the bar and tried to stay as hidden as possible so as not to feel their gaze. One of the police officers joined them after a while.

Xena calmed down; it was obvious that they were his clients. Her calm did not last long. The three men talked and looked at her. It became clear to her that she was the topic of the conversation. Xena looked around; the cafe was half empty. In addition to the table with the three men, there were two other clients. One was a regular customer at this time of the day, the other was a woman Xena had never seen before. The woman didn't stay long. She left after a quick sip of her coffee.

The police officer talking to his clients got up from his chair and headed for Xena. She instinctively stepped back slightly.

'Hello,' he said.

'Hello,' she replied.

He studied her. He must have sensed her concern.

'These two gentlemen have an offer for you,' he finally said.

'Tell them I'm not interested,' she said.

'But you don't know what the offer is.'

'I can guess,' she said, turning her back on him. Xena entered the kitchen. He walked behind the bar and followed her. He grabbed her elbow roughly and pulled her close.

'They offer good rewards for just a few hours with you.' His voice was insistent, his face millimetres from hers and she could feel his breath. Xena tried to free herself, but he pulled her even closer to him. He grabbed her face and turned it so that he met her gaze.

'I don't know who you are but working in this bar means that you are hiding something. I'll check you and put you behind bars if you don't do what I want.'

Xena withdrew her hand, and said, 'I'm not afraid of you. I have nothing to hide.'

He did not answer and began to search her rudely. He rummaged in her pockets and even put his hand in her bra. When he didn't find what he needed, he looked around. He picked up her phone, examined it and tossed it on the counter. Then his gaze fell on her jacket. He was looking for something, but Xena didn't know what. He searched her pockets and smiled when he saw the ID. The ID was not Xena's, it was Dary's roommate, but the police officer had no way of knowing that.

'Anna Ivanova?' he wondered. 'I thought your name was Xena.'

'Xena was a childhood nickname,' she said, looking at him intently. She was dizzy. All this stress was beginning to affect her.

'All right, Anna. I'll take your ID and see what you're hiding.'

There was a slight rustle behind the bar. The client Xena had left alone approached and pulled the ID card from the officer's hand.

'You won't see anything,' he said.

'But...' the police officer began.

'Xena works for me, Petkov. She's our bartender, she's not one of your girls. Take your customers and leave. You will find them another woman who agrees to the deal. This one here already has a job. Her job is to take care of the peace of your and our clients. Do you understand?'

'I understand, Mr. Chief.'

The chief handed Xena her ID and returned to the table. The two men headed for the door, the police officer left money on the table and looked at Xena. There was nothing good in his eyes. Xena felt as if snakes had bitten her. Her body trembled but she tried to cover it up. She started cleaning around and never knew when the chief had left. Apparently, this was Svetla's husband. An unassuming middle-aged man until he acted. Then he showed his strength. Xena had experience with people, she could almost always tell from a small conversation if they were good or bad, but this man was a mystery to her. He looked like an office worker, there was nothing to suggest he was a law enforcement officer. The police officers and especially those above them, had a slightly haughty appearance, their gait, their actions, their speech - all this betrayed them. Not this man. He could pass for anyone. Calm and balanced, that was what scared her. He had protected her, but at the same time he had shown her that she belonged to him. Instead of feeling relieved, she felt threatened. Her hands trembled and she dropped two glasses, and they smashed on the floor. She felt trapped, from which she didn't know how to escape.

Svetla had hired her because she probably knew who she really was. Her husband must have learned that Xena was wanted for murder. As the police officer said, it was no accident that she worked in this bar.

The cafe slowly began to fill for lunch, but Xena decided to make coffee and sit behind the bar to calm down and think. What happened today upset her. What did Svetla and her husband know about her, she wondered. Her hands wrapped around the glass, and she was relieved to see that they were no longer trembling. She finished her coffee, put her cup in the dishwasher and went back to work.

In the evening she received an email from Dary. She wanted to see her as soon as possible. She had something to tell her. Xena decided to meet Dary on Sunday. She opened her laptop and instead of learning English, as she had done for the past few months, this time she opened the search engine and looked for information about Ivan's murder.

There were no official suspects in his murder. The information was scarce, an investigation was underway. There was a picture of the investigating inspector. Xena knew him, he often came to the nightclub talking with criminals. He was one of Long One's men and everyone in the small town knew about it. As she read the details of her ex-boyfriend's death, Xena was moved. She began to remember events in their lives. Her face was covered with tears. She missed Ivan. He was one of her closest people, it was only now, at that moment, that she realised that he was indeed dead. Until now, she seemed to refuse to accept that fact. She always thought it was a scam to find her, but for several months now the information has been confirmed. The last thing Xena read was that the case was being referred to the District Police. A new, more thorough investigation would begin, and they would try to find the culprit for Ivan's death. What had reassured her somewhat was that the investigation would continue. What worried her was that her escape could be interpreted as an escape from a crime scene. She couldn't prove otherwise. She couldn't find out on the Internet exactly when Ivan's death occurred, but if it had been the same night she was hiding in Dora's house, and they would have easily attributed the murder to her. Now she remembered that she had left the bloody clothes in the house, she had left them in the attic and although she was sure that they would not find Ivan's DNA on them, she did not know how the events could be interpreted.

Xena closed the laptop and curled up on the bed. Strong convulsions shook her body. Tears began to flow again. Her sobs were quiet, trying not to get her roommates' attention. She was so lonely, and she was also terrified. A few hours later Xena relaxed on the bed. She would keep working at the bar while she could. It was her protection, though she knew it was a double-edged sword. Xena felt the urge to run again. She had rarely done so since she had come to Sofia, but this morning she put on her sportswear and new trainers and went outside. It was dawn outside and it was her favourite time for jogging.

An hour later she returned sweaty and tired. Her fatigue was pleasant, she could feel the drops of sweat running down her back. While she was running, she decided to start self-defence lessons. She had to find a karate club nearby. She would not allow anyone else to physically control her. What happened at the bar yesterday hit her hard and she had found a solution. She would learn to fight, to fight for her freedom not only morally and mentally, but also physically.

After taking a quick shower, Xena went to work at the bar. Two of the prostitutes were waiting for her at the door. Their friendship was gone, they looked at her hostilely and Xena knew the reason. They were two of the policeman's girls. Apparently, they considered it a competition. Xena spoke first.

'I don't want to have anything to do with him if that's what you came here to discuss.'

The two women looked at each other.

'Right? And why is he only talking about you? You failed one of his best deals.'

'Ask him for an explanation, not me. I am a bartender, I sell food and drinks, not my body.'

'You think you are smart, huh?' one of the women asked.

'No. I'm telling you the truth.'

'If you get close to him again, you'll be sorry.'

The two ladies left the cafe. They passed with another friend of theirs.

'If you came to threaten me, you can follow them. I don't want to have anything to do with your pimp,' Xena told her.

'No, I actually came to drink coffee in peace. Or tea.'

Xena walked behind the bar and made two coffees. She carried them to the table and sat down with the woman. She examined her closely and found that they didn't really differ much in age or physique.

'Excuse my friends. They are nervous. Yesterday, someone offered three times the price for you than they offered them. Did you really refuse?'

'Yes, I refused.'

'They would pay good money for just a few hours of attention, a little sex. There is nothing wrong with that.'

'What is your name?' Xena asked her.

'My name is Irina and I found out that your real name is Anna.'

Xena did not answer. She put some sugar in her coffee and began stirring with a spoon.

'I know it's just sex for you, but I can't understand. How can you be with a man you don't know? How can you be with someone you have no feelings for?'

'Ah, of course, you're a moral, sensual one,' Irina said. 'Now I understand why you refused. This job is not for everyone. It wasn't for me either. The first time was terrible, the second time too. Then you get used to it, you play a role.'

'A role?' Xena asked.

'Yes, you pretend that you like what you do, but in fact, it is not so. I already forgot what it's like to make love. I really loved the man who got me involved. I was enchanted. I did everything he told me, and I did it because I loved him so much.'

'Why don't you give up and find someone who really loves you?' Xena asked her.

'And do you have someone who really loves you?' Irina answered her question with a question.

Xena thought for a moment, paused, and said, 'No, I don't.'

'Here, you see. We have something in common. You're a bartender, I'm a companion, but we both lack the same thing. Trust and love.'

Xena stared at the woman across from her. She was smart, incredibly beautiful, and young. She came to the wrong place at the wrong time and went the wrong way. The two remained at the table for a few more minutes, finished their coffee in silence, then new customers arrived and broke the silence.

3

RUN, RUN AND RUN

On Sunday Xena headed to meet Dary. They hadn't seen each other in months. Xena couldn't wait to see her. For a short time Dary had become her most trusted person. Xena went to the meeting a little earlier, ordered tea and waited. She looked at the people around her and wondered how they lived. Were they happy or unhappy? Were they loved? Then she saw Dary in the distance. Dary was wearing a blue sports jacket with her bag slung over her shoulder. She looked like a teenager with a slightly nervous smile. Xena wondered what was bothering her friend. Her usual radiance was not present now.

Dary sat down next to her and ordered an espresso. Apparently, she was coming after a night shift.

'Nice to see you,' she told Xena. 'You look good.'

'And you look worried and tired,' Xena said, smiling at her friend.

'I'm just back from a night shift and I'm sleepy.'

'Why didn't you tell me? I could've seen you later today,' Xena asked her.

'It's no problem. I will be fine after drinking a cup of coffee.'

Dary leaned back in her chair and settled more comfortably.

'I should have seen you and talked to you,' she said.

'What's up, what's happened?' Xena asked worried.

'You were right about the phone. They followed me.'

'They were looking for me at your place, weren't they?' Xena asked.

'No, they were looking for you at the hospital. A man from your hometown. He said he was from the police, but I don't know why I didn't believe him.'

'What did the man look like?' Xena asked.

After Dary's description, Xena was sure he was the inspector from her hometown, Long One's man.

'What did you tell him?'

'That you asked to use my phone to send a message. I told him that you were out of the hospital the next day and that I don't know where you are now.'

'When did this happen?'

'More than a month ago. I didn't want to contact you in case they didn't believe me and followed me.'

'All right. What did he tell you?'

'That they're looking for you for your ex-boyfriend's murder and that you are their first suspect.'

'Yesterday I checked on the Internet, I am not a suspect in the murder, not officially.'

'That's what the other one told me.'

'There was another one?' Xena asked in surprise.

'Another inspector came a week later. He was actually a civilian and introduced himself as an Inspector from the District Prosecutor's Office. He actually said another abbreviated name of an agency, but I don't remember it. He said they are now leading the investigation and are looking for a key witness, not a defendant.'

'And what did you tell him?' Xena asked.

'The same as the other, although he didn't seem to believe me when I told him I hadn't seen you again.'

Xena looked ahead thoughtfully.

'He left me a business card and told me that if I happened to meet you, I should give it to you so you can call him.'

Dary handed the business card to Xena. The name Daniel Dobrevski was written on it. This name sounded familiar to her, but she couldn't remember exactly what the connection was. Xena entered the phone number in her phone contacts and returned the business card to Dary.

'Hold onto it and in case of an emergency, call him. I don't know if he is the one, he claims to be, but it was written on the Internet that the case was transferred to the District Prosecutor's Office. Can you describe what he looks like?' Xena asked.

'Yes. Handsome, with black hair, dark brown eyes, tall and strong. He catches the eye.' Dary grinned foolishly.

'I avoid the handsome boys,' Xena said. 'There will always be another woman who wants him. He will never be completely mine. Although now that I think about it, Ivan was handsome too.'

'Do you miss him?'

'Yes. Yesterday, while reading the information about his case, I remembered how much we were in love as teenagers.' Xena's burst into tears. 'I still don't understand what happened to him. Why did he get us in this mess? It's hard for me to believe I won't see him again.'

Dary tried to reassure her friend, 'You have to look ahead now. Will you call this inspector?'

'No. He may be one of the men from my town. If he asks you about me again, don't tell him we've seen each other. I will try to check who he really is.'

'All right. I have to go. I feel very tired,' Dary said.

'And you look tired. I'm sorry I got you involved.'

'Don't be sorry. I will let you know if there is anything else. I hope to see you soon.'

The two women hugged. Dary walked slowly to the bus stop and Xena paused for a moment, wondering how lucky she was to have a friend like Dary. She wouldn't be able to survive without her. Neither when she arrived, nor now.

Xena arrived home tired. Everything from her past was bothering her and making her cry. She decided to see if she could find any information about Daniel Dobrevski. She typed his name into the search engine. There were several social media accounts with that name, but they were either young or blonde men. Apparently Mr. Dobrevski didn't want anyone to know about him. Her search led nowhere. This calmed her down somewhat. People around Long One liked to be on display. Maybe this inspector was who he said he was. Xena closed her laptop. She didn't know who to trust and who not to. For now, the only person she trusted was Dary.

The next morning, she opened the cafe early than usual. She couldn't stay at home. For some reason she wanted to be among people. She was just making coffee when the door opened and Svetla came in and locked it behind her.

'We need to talk,' she told her.

Svetla was visibly worried, which was not her usual state. She was usually a woman of self-confidence and strength. Xena's intuition suggested there was a problem. She hoped it had nothing to do with what happened a few days ago.

'Sit down,' she told her boss. 'Do you want me to make you a coffee?'

'Yes, thank you.'

Xena made her a coffee and sat down.

'I understand you met my husband.'

Xena nodded.

'He's one of the Police Chiefs. He has been in that position for a long time and apparently someone wants to replace him. There are various rumours from different sides that they will check both his bank accounts and the activities of the cafe. Fortunately, from the very beginning we were advised to have everything in my name. What I wanted to talk to you about is you have to be careful. Make a receipt for each sale, clean more often and don't talk to anyone about the side businesses that are organised here.'

'All right,' Xena said. 'You look scared.'

'I don't know what to expect and where, so I came to talk to you. Has anyone questioned you on any occasion?'

'No. In most cases, I am a listener, not a talker.'

'Good to know. That was the reason we hired you. You are discreet. Still, be careful. We expect the inspection to last one or two weeks. If they find nothing, they will leave us alone. Of course, we will increase your salary. Can I count on you?'

'I won't tell anyone but if someone comes and starts creating problems, what should I do?'

'Call me. If I don't answer, leave a message in my voicemail.'

'All right. I hope it will not be necessary.'

Svetla finished her coffee and left the cafe.

Another mess, Xena thought. There was tension for the next few days. Everyone looked around anxiously as they entered and relieved as they left the cafe. At the end of the week everything went back to normal. On Sunday, Xena managed to rest, all this stress began to affect her. She decided to buy a book and go home to read. Her day passed imperceptibly. Curled up on the bed with a book in hand and a peppermint tea, Xena finally felt calmer.

She opened the cafe just in time on Monday morning. She was just making coffee for herself when three men came in and locked the door with a table. There was no other way out of the cafe and Xena felt like a trapped mouse. She started to pick up the phone, but one of the men shook his head slowly. Understanding his gesture, she hung up and waited.

'There's no point in trying to run or shout. There is no one around, we checked.'

Xena didn't answer, she waited.

'We are from the Tax Inspectorate. We need all the documents at the cafe.'

'Would you give me your ID?' Xena said.

'Of course.'

The three men pulled out their ID cards and said their names.

'And now the documents,' said one of them.

Xena handed them the folders in which all the certificates, contracts, payments were carefully attached. She knew that everything in this folder was clean. Svetla's accountant had taken care of everything.

'You can call the owners now if you want them to attend the inspection.'

Xena called Sveta and left a voice message, as she had been told before.

'We'll need your documents, too. Contracts and identity card.'

'My contract is in the folder. Here is my ID card.'

'Anna, is that your name?'

'Yes. '

'Do you have any siblings?'

'I have a brother. Xena had asked Dary for personal information from her ex-roommate. She hoped she wouldn't be questioned much because she didn't know anything else about Anna.'

The men leaned over the documents and began to check them one by one. Xena sat in the chair behind the bar pretending to drink coffee. Everything in her trembled. She couldn't wait for

Svetla to come and deal with the mess here, but two hours passed, and she didn't come.

'Will you show me the gaming machine documents?' one of the men asked her.

'All the documents are in the folder,' she said.

'They are not there,' he said. His gaze was insistent.

'Okay, I'll look behind the bar for them in case they fell out.'

Xena checked everywhere, but she didn't find any more documents.

'Have you ever seen documents for these machines?'

'Yes, there were three documents, one for each machine,' she lied.

The man approached the machines and began to inspect them, finding what he needed. It was a number. He took a picture of it and returned to the others. He opened his laptop and began writing something.

'These machines are not registered. Do you know what the penalty is for illegal roulette?' he asked her.

'No, but I'm sure they are legal.'

'In addition to a fine, there is a prison sentence of up to three years.'

Xena turned pale. They must have registered the slot machines, she thought. They were expecting an inspection.

'You're in trouble, Anna,' he said.

The three men turned to her.

'I have nothing to do with this.'

'How could you not? You work here, don't you?'

'Yes, but I don't deal with the documents.'

'Your contract says you are a manager. Is that correct?'

Xena was speechless. Her contract was for a bartender. Unless someone had changed it.

'It says here that you are a manager,' one man handed her the document.

'Yes,' she said at last, 'but my boss was in charge of the permits.'

'Did you call her? Will she come?'

'I couldn't connect. I left her a voice mail.'

'We can't wait for her. You are a manager. We will draw up an act and give you the opportunity to provide the necessary documents within forty-eight hours. Do you understand?'

'Yes, I do understand.'

The three men buried themselves in the computers again, one of them typing, the others dictating. Using a small printer, they printed a document that prompted her to sign. The document said nothing different from what she had been told.

'If you don't show up within forty-eight hours with the documents, we will bring you to justice. My advice is to find your bosses and talk to them about the situation.'

Then they left. They left the door open, and people immediately entered the cafe. Xena kept calling Svetla, but no one came or contacted her until late in the afternoon. She wondered what to do, drop everything and leave or stay until the end of the shift.

Svetla finally came. She didn't explain why she was late. After the last client left, Xena settled down next to Svetla. Her boss had scattered documents all over the table.

'Do we have that permit?' Xena asked.

'No, we don't.'

'What are we going to do?'

'You'll go tomorrow afternoon and talk to them.'

'What can I tell them?'

'I'll ask someone, and I'll let you know tomorrow.'

Svetla didn't look worried, but Xena was. She returned to her room, took a shower, and began to search for information about the document they demanded. The consequences for her if she didn't present the document would be greater than for her bosses. She tried to sleep, but she was restless all night. Finally, at five in the morning, she got up and made herself a coffee. Xena drank it slowly, waited for the sun to rise and went out to run. Running was her therapy. It treated her stress. She ran for more than an hour and a half, came back terribly tired, took a quick shower, changed, and headed for the cafe. Two men were waiting at the cafe door. One looked like a bad guy and his gaze was frightening her. The other seemed more balanced and calmer, but Xena saw that there was a tic on his cheek and guessed that his calm was only apparent. She pretended not to be bothered by their appearance. Walked past them and headed for the entrance.

'I'll open in fifteen minutes,' she told them.

They didn't answer. The moment she opened the door, they pushed her roughly into the room.

'Call your boss,' said the angry one.

Xena did as she was told. However, Svetla did not answer the call.

'What's happening?' Xena asked. 'What do you want?'

One man pushed her against the wall, squeezed her neck and whispered in her ear.

'You'll find out soon enough.'

The men dragged her to one of the end tables and began talking to each other. They spoke Serbian or Croatian, she understood to some extent what they were saying but not everything. They were arguing over whether to release her when her boss came or to detain her. Xena was silent, unwilling to interrupt the argument and turn their attention back to herself. She jumped when the phone rang. Svetla returned her call. The larger man removed her hand from the phone and answered. They spoke a foreign language, but this time Xena didn't understand what it was all about. However, the man got nervous, blushed, and threw the phone into the other part of the room. Xena's body froze. She felt the angry looks of the men. One of them pushed her angrily to the floor and started hitting her. He hit her in the face first. She felt dizzy, writhed in pain, and tried to cover her face with her hands. She failed to cover it in time and a second strong blow stunned her.

Tears began to flow down her cheeks. She couldn't hide them. The pain was very strong, she was blinded and all she saw were red spots. Xena was trying to get out, looking for support or something to swing, but she was blind. She saw nothing. The blows stopped. She heard an argument between the two men. They began to fight among themselves, but it was more wrestling than a real fight. Xena heard the door unlock and someone seemed to leave. She felt the breath of someone near her.

'I'm sorry about that,' the man said. 'My partner is uncontrollable sometimes. It's not your fault and he know it. The police will confiscate the slots if we leave them here, so we'll take them now. Don't move or say anything so I don't have to save you again.'

Xena nodded. She rested her head on the floor and pretended not to hear what was happening around her. The men took the machines but before they left the angry man smashed everything he could and stepped on her hand to show her that his anger was not over. Xena cried out in pain. The man's entire weight landed on her fragile wrist, and he pressed hard, watching her writhe. Xena tried not to shout so as not to provoke him to do something else. She recalled how, while wandering in the woods, a hunter told them how he had escaped death when he was attacked by a bear. He pretended to be dead. He did his best not to move or breathe. That's what she did now. She relaxed her muscles and pretended to be unconscious. These types of men take pleasure in feeling your pain. Once she fainted, he lost interest in her. The men came out and left her lying on the floor. The door to the cafe remained open.

Two minutes later one of her clients helped her to get up on her feet. She refused the ambulance. Xena didn't want to go to the hospital again. She would manage on her own. She wrote a message to Svetla that they had taken the machines, then locked the cafe and tried to get better. Everything was hurting, especially her head. Xena hoped she would recover quickly. She had to. If she didn't go to the taxmen, there would be more trouble than the fight.

Xena turned on the hot tap water in the kitchen and waited for it to heat up. She found the first aid kit and took care of her wounds. Her hand was hurt very badly, she put ice on it and attached the ice with a rag from the bar. She jumped again when her phone rang.

'What happened?' Svetla asked.

'They took the machines. There was nothing I could do.'

'Will you unlock the door for me?' Svetla was obviously trying to enter but Xena had left the key on the inside of the door. She unlocked it and met her boss' critical gaze.

'What happened to you?' Svetla asked.

'One of them hit me several times.'

'You have to go to the hospital.' Svetla looked at her worriedly.

'It's not necessary,' Xena said.

Svetla took ice from the freezer and began helping her apply it to her wounds. It may be able to prevent bruising.

'Xena, I'm sorry about what has happened in the last few days,' she said sincerely. 'I never intended to involve you in anything.'

'What exactly is happening? I still don't understand why?', Xena asked her.

'Some people want to disable our business. They are attacking us as best as they can. Someone called the tax office and told them to look for documents for the slot machines. Yesterday he called those who rented us the machine and told them that we had given them all the information about them. Their business is illegal and that's why they got nervous.'

'Well. Okay. Can we get out of this mess?' Xena asked. It was hard for her to think, her head was throbbing, but she had to do her best to get out of it.

'Probably. You will go and talk to the tax authorities. If all goes well, we will pay you six months' salary in advance and we will let you leave.'

'What if it doesn't go well?' Xena's voice betrayed her tension.

'It must go well. I'm sure you can handle it,' Svetla didn't answer the question directly. 'Now rest, we have three hours to prepare you.'

Svetla began to clean the glass pieces from the floor. At that moment, a woman arrived who introduced herself as Ina. In the middle of the conversation with her, Xena realised that she was also from the tax office. The woman told her not only what to say, but also how to behave. At noon Svetla made them sandwiches. Xena's head ached badly, not only from the blows inflicted on her, but from all the information she had to remember. Ina prepared her very well. It was her appearance. One of the girls brought makeup. She did her best to hide the swelling and injuries on Xena's skin. When Xena saw herself in the mirror, she couldn't recognise herself. The makeup had changed her and yet she was the same.

Before leaving, she took a painkiller and drank a tea to relax her nerves.

Svetla and Ina accompanied her to the building and told her to call the two men.

The men received her in a small office full of documents. They seemed to be expecting her. They were of different ages; the younger one was like a newer copy of the old one. His manners, way of expression, had absorbed everything from his older colleague. The only difference between the two was skin colour. One had profuse redness, which Xena guessed was from decades of alcohol abuse. The other had a healthy and youthful appearance, but with signs of a growing belly. Apparently, neither of them took good care of their health.

The younger one smiled at Xena.

'You changed your appearance in just a few hours,' he commented.

Xena did not answer.

'Do you have the documents?' the older man asked, not impressed by her appearance.

'No,' she said shortly.

'Then why are you here?'

Xena began to recite everything she was told to say. The meeting lasted about half an hour. Eventually, she was allowed to leave without being charged or prosecuted. It was all in her head, Ina had said. It was important to feel confident in the answers and not allow yourself to be pressured.

Xena left the building and took a deep breath. She felt as if a heavy burden had fallen from her shoulders. She looked at the corner of the next building and met Svetla. She smiled at her. Svetla returned her smile. Xena still couldn't understand how and why this good and lively woman was engaged in illegal transactions and became involved with criminals and swindlers.

Svetla hugged her and said, 'From the moment I saw you, I knew you were a brave girl. You fulfilled the deal, now it's my turn.'

She reached into her handbag and pulled out a plastic bag.

'Use the money wisely, get a good job and try to stay away from police stations. Many police officers know you and will probably try to take advantage of this. Rest for a few months and if you have dizziness go to the doctor. I don't want to find out that you fainted somewhere.'

Svetla started to leave, but Xena stopped her.

'Why? Why are you doing all this?' she asked.

'It's a long story, you don't have to know it, but I'm already involved in it and unlike you, I can't get away. One has consequences for one's actions and words, remember that. Sooner or later, everything you did against your soul and your heart will return to you. So only do what you think is right. Do not get involved in things that you may regret later.'

'It's a little late,' Xena said softly. Want it or not, she was already involved not in one but two messes.

4

ALONE AMONG THE PEOPLE

Xena took Svetla's advice and stayed home for two weeks. Her head hadn't hurt in a long time. She didn't go out much, she stayed more in her room and even avoided her roommates. She followed the news just in case they said anything about Svetla and her husband but there was no information about them.

Xena delved into learning English. All she wanted was to get out of the country. She no longer felt safe in Sofia. She had nightmares. She couldn't sleep and locked the door to her room every time she was alone. She was afraid of strangers and expected to be attacked, even as she walked down the street. People didn't pay attention to her. They often passed her without noticing her. Xena knew that fear was not healthy, she read a lot about the subject on the Internet, but she couldn't get rid of the feeling that someone was suffocating her. She had two high-collar blouses in her meagre wardrobe and threw them away, she couldn't wear them. Xena couldn't even wear a necklace. She realised that it would be difficult to overcome this fear, so she bought some books. She read all day, different genres, different stories, but nothing with a lot of violence and murder. After some hesitation, she looked for a karate club nearby. She didn't know what to expect, martial arts were unlikely to heal this trauma, but she sincerely hoped to at least blunt it.

Surprisingly for her after two training sessions she found that she was calmer. Karate consisted not only of fighting techniques, but also of meditation and training the soul and spirit. During training no one asked her who she was, what she did or where she lived. The only information they asked from her was about her health.

A month after parting with Svetla, Xena felt ready to return to normal life. It took her longer than she expected, but she felt fresh and less frightened now. She had to take matters into her own hands and continue her life. This is the advice of all experts on the Internet. Not that she believed everything she read.

Before looking for a new job Xena wanted to meet Dary again. They had exchanged several emails, but she missed her friend.

They met in a busy place, on one of the main streets, full of restaurants and cafes. Just in case, Xena had put on a little more makeup than usual to make her eyes a little longer. It was a sign that she was still afraid, but she tried to ignore the thought.

Dary was a few minutes late. Unlike last time, now she looked rested and somehow happy. Xena felt a big change in her friend's mood and appearance. Her friend's eyes shone, her lips smiled mysteriously, and her voice was alive. There was no doubt that she had met someone special.

The two women hugged and looked at each other.

'You look amazing,' Xena said. 'Who is responsible for this?'

'Nothing can be hidden from you,' Dary laughed. 'The reason is a colleague.'

'A workplace relationship. Is that not dangerous?' Xena interjected.

'No, it's exciting,' Dary said again laughing. Her brown hair fluttered carelessly and tangled in her neck, but she ignored it. Everything in her shone.

'Ah, love, love,' Xena said in a low mood, 'I want to feel it again.'

'I'm sure you will. One day you will meet the amazing man who deserves you. By the way, one doesn't stop coming and asking about you.'

'Who? 'Xena regained her fear.

'The handsome one I told you about last time.'

'Why is he asking you about me again? You told him you didn't know where I was.'

'I told him, but he insists that if I see you one day, I should tell you to contact him. He gave me two more business cards in a month.'

'Do you think he followed you?'

'Now? No, there is no way. I slept at my new friend's house.'

'Oh, you've already moved to another home?'

'Yes, after a moment's hesitation.'

'And how is it?'

'Very good. He is a wonderful man. I really want to introduce you, but I know it's better for you not to meet a lot of people. I didn't tell him about you. I told him I was going to the market. Men hate shopping and he is no exception.'

'My ex obviously didn't hate shopping. I still wonder what he spent all that money on. Anyway. I signed up to practice karate.'

'Really? Great. It will work well for you.'

'It's starting to work well for me already.'

'Well,' Dary returned to the subject, 'why don't you call the inspector? See what he has to say to you, he looks like a good man. Although nowadays the bad guys manage to hide.'

'Will you describe him to me again?'

'Yes, this time I got a better look at him. I wanted to take a photo, but I couldn't. He is tall, dark-haired, with large brown eyes and dark eyebrows. He certainly trains regularly. His hair is cut short but not military. All three times he has worn jeans and a t-shirt. What do you think, do you know who he is?'

'I don't know. I researched information about him on the Internet but there is no such person. I know his last name, we had a family on our street with that last name, but there is no way he can be one of them. They moved a long time ago, but somehow his name worries me. He can present himself as a police inspector. I'm afraid to contact him. I don't know how to explain...'

'You might be right. Maybe I'm not cautious and as you know I am naive. I want to help you figure out who he is, but I don't know how.'

'Don't worry about it. I'll find out who he is somehow,' Xena said, not very convincingly.

'Are you okay?' Dary asked, looking at her friend quizzically.

'I'm fine.'

'Everything shows that you are not well, but I sincerely hope you get better soon,' Dary said.

They talked for another hour about fashion, politics and everything that was happening around them and then parted, hoping to see each other soon and under better circumstances for Xena.

Xena didn't share with Dary what had happened in the cafe. She didn't want to bother her any more than she already had, and now was not the time to share such disturbing information. Her friend was happy and in love. She had to let her enjoy the moment. Xena couldn't wait to meet Dary's boyfriend, but Dary was right, she had to be careful with who she met. If this police inspector kept looking for her, even the smallest thing could lead him to her.

Xena returned to her room, instinctively locking her door. She heard a noise in the house and knew she was not alone, but with her roommates. She opened her laptop and started looking for a job. It was time to merge in with the crowd.

She got up early again in the morning, went for a long jog and returned with breakfast. As she ran, she examined the trees and was surprised to find that it was already autumn. Her favourite season. Now the mountain in Vedna would be painted in beautiful autumn colours, from bright yellow to bright red. She missed the view of her favourite peaks, she wanted to leave for at least a few hours and climb high, then stay on top and watch the view below. Unfortunately, that couldn't happen, and Xena exerted her efforts in search of work. She applied to several places and by noon she had scheduled two interviews.

Xena decided to work at night. She hadn't thought about it before, but the chance of someone recognising her in a nightclub if she wore more makeup would be less than the chance if she worked somewhere during the day. That's why she focused on searching for a night job.

For the first two days, she couldn't find anything suitable. She didn't just want to start a job somewhere, she had to like the atmosphere and the owner and the ones she'd seen so far were definitely not the best. On the contrary, they talked to her arrogantly, taking money and jewellery to the table, perhaps to impress her. Although, the pay they offered didn't sound impressive. These men were men with complexes, and she definitely had no intention of working for them. The money Svetla had given her would be enough for seven or eight months, allowing her to choose where to work without worrying and being pressed by the time.

On the fifth day, she went to a nightclub called *'Kill Me'*. Before she came, she wasn't sure if she would like to work in a club with that name, but the moment she walked in and heard the laughter of staff members, she changed her mind. People did not smile so sincerely at work. Her curiosity grew when she saw the situation. It was pleasant, not fancy, without shiny gold and silver ornaments. Everything was made of soft colours. It looked like a nightclub, but everything indicated that it was a club with class above the others. The furniture was not soft, the tables were non-standard shapes, the countertops were made of resin which was in vogue at the moment. The chairs were high bar stools. When she sat down on one of them, she found that they were comfortable, but they would not allow drunken people to linger on them for long.

Apparently, that's how the owner had decided to deal with sleeping customers. They could hardly sleep in a highchair for long. The clients either kept drinking or left and allowed another customer to sit in the seat. Xena liked the way the owner thought before she even met him. However, his appearance surprised her even more.

'I suppose you're Xena,' said a pimpled young man.

'Yes. I have an appointment for an interview with the owner.'

The young man smiled.

'I'm the owner. My name is Galin, but everyone calls me Gal.'

Xena's surprise was evident. She tried to cover it up, but Gal waved and said, 'Everyone reacts like that and before you ask me, I'm an adult. I turned twenty-one two months ago. I inherited some money when I was eighteen years old and since by law I could sell and drink alcohol, I opened a bar. The business took off and here I am, although no one, not even me, expected it to last.'

Xena really liked Gal. He was young, smiling, and lively. Nothing to do with other nightclub owners. Gal was nice and Xena was sure that once the pimples were gone, he would become a very handsome man. She was twenty-eight years old, which meant that her boss would be seven years younger than her. She had never worked for anyone younger than her before. All her bosses were much older. She liked Gal very much. He was with a good sense of humour and an obviously calm character. Apparently, he liked her too. He asked her to show him what she could do, asked her a few questions, then they talked for almost an hour about common things. The waiters joked about him, but you could still feel the respect everyone had for him.

'So, Xena, what do you think of my nightclub?'

'It's great. I don't know what the nightclub will look like at night, but I'm impressed. Only its name worries me.'

'You can come tonight and see for yourself what night-time will look like, as for my club's name, it seemed original to me,' he said with a smile. 'What do you think girls, do you think she can join our club?'

'Yes,' everyone replied in unison.

Xena left in good spirits. It was too good to be true, she thought, but her intuition told her that these people were good. She returned home, changed and for the first time in a while she didn't lock the door to her room. She left for training with a smile. She couldn't wait to go to work that evening.

Xena liked the nightclub at night. The music was loud, the lights changed colour, a mist suffused. In that twilight she hoped no one would recognise her. Her colleagues quickly introduced her to the job. She felt like she had worked there all her life. The nightclub was a good cover for her, and this removed some of her fears. She was almost certain that illegal business was not going on here or at least not with the consent of the owner.

Xena had arranged with Gal for six working days or nights. The pay he had offered her was more than she had expected. The tips were also shared equally between the bartenders and waiters and turned out to be a decent income, but that's not all Xena liked. The working hours were while there were customers, but most of them left by three in the morning and that suited her. Gal had arranged transportation for the staff, which gave Xena peace of mind, she was not worried about how she would get home. She was in the right place, at the right time. She couldn't believe that life this time was giving to her, not taking from her.

In a short time, Xena befriended all her colleagues but to her surprise Gal talked to her the most. At first, she thought he was studying her but after a while she saw his sincere interest in her. Every night he greeted her at work with hot bitter coffee and told her jokes and stories. After a while, he felt like a friend. He said he had no friends, and she was filling that void. One day he told Xena that she, like him, looked alone among many people. She agreed with him. She felt lonely, not alone, but lonely. He was definitely a busy young man, surrounded by many people around him, but he was right, all his conversations revolved around work. The same people every week, hugs and stories that were without much content and he, like her, did not look alone, but lonely. Xena thought he probably had friends before he opened the bar and asked him once. Gal answered evasively. She also didn't talk about relatives and friends, but he did not question her. He seemed to know her secret. Although she was sure he couldn't really.

Xena continued to run every morning and went to karate practice three times per week. Over time, she became stronger, more confident, and flexible as she walked. She walked with a slightly raised step. Kata, which is part of karate, taught her to concentrate. Her sense of self changed. Sometimes she looked in the mirror and didn't recognise herself. From a gentle young woman, she had become an athletic young woman. Her efforts paid off, she no longer looked so vulnerable, and she realised it. Conscious femininity. She had read about it in a book. Her life had changed, or she had changed her life, but deep down in her soul, she still felt hurt. She was still afraid of the future and worried about the past. There was a string inside her that couldn't change and couldn't break. She had to hold it and be careful not to touch it or make a sound.

The days and nights passed quickly. Xena had a routine and followed it every day. She usually took a day off during the week because there was a lot of work at the bar on the weekends. She loved spending her days off outside, walking in the park, shopping, generally wandering almost carefree and for the first time in her life she felt free and happy. Of course, she often had nightmares at night, still wore nothing around her neck and no matter how much she liked scarves, she was sickened at the sight of them. Maybe she would carry that burden for years. Although she felt calm at work, she sometimes looked at customers and expected someone to attack her. It was good that the dimness and the intermittent lights obscured her.

Gal caught the look in her eyes at times, but he always smiled reassuringly and that was enough for Xena to dull her fear. Gal once asked her if she was afraid of anyone. She told him she was afraid of many things. This young man seemed to understand her. She knew nothing about his past, but like him she felt something was wrong. He covered himself with a smile with every attempt from people who tried to understand where he came from and how he received this legacy, which he often spoke of. Two loners of different ages, it was the two of them. One too young, Xena thought.

Gal, on the other hand, was in love with Xena. He tried to be friendly with her. He saw that she was scared of something, and he was sure she was mostly afraid of the presence of a certain type of man. He tried several times to find out what had happened, but she, like him, had learned to answer questions with a question. Xena was a very beautiful woman, but the strangest thing was that she didn't even realise it. There were a few men who looked at her, many invited her on a date, but she always refused without even thinking about it. She said one of the clichés about bonding with colleagues or clients, and then she quickly got out of the situation. That's why Gal didn't know how to explain his feelings to her. He was worried about her answering him with another cliché or worse. So, he stood at a distance, making sure she felt calm, clearly hoping that the day would come when she would look at him with different eyes, not as a friend and boss. All he had to do was wait and he was ready for a long wait.

It had been a few months since Xena started working at the nightclub. The days passed calmly and monotonously. It was winter, the nights were long and the days short. This forced Xena to start work earlier because the customers left earlier. The snow outside had covered the streets, the traffic was a nightmare but that didn't bother her. On her day off, she decided to take a walk. She went into a small bookstore and then she saw him. A tall handsome man, just as Dary described him. There was something familiar about him but again she couldn't remember what it was. He walked over to her and started talking to her. Xena turned her head and gestured to the bookseller. She asked him a few questions, walking lightly toward the door as she spoke to him. Then she ran quickly. The bookseller held his breath and the handsome man tried to catch up with her. Thanks to her daily training, Xena managed to escape. She sneaked into the crowd and continued with a slow calm gait so as not to attract attention. She walked to her apartment, turning from time to time to see if anyone was watching her. Her heart was beating fast. Her adrenaline rose. She leaned back on her bed and tried to calm down.

He had found her.

But who was he, she wondered? He wasn't hostile and yes, Dary was right, he was handsome. Something was bothering her, but she couldn't figure out who he reminded her of. After about an hour, Xena's breathing calmed. At least now she knew what he looked like, she thought. Xena often went to this bookstore, apparently her routine had betrayed her. She had to be careful in the future and keep training, but it was time to change her karate club. Also, the shops she had visited before. It would be better to shop from a more remote place. She had just decided that her life had returned to normal, and everything reminded her for just a moment that she would never have a normal life. She had to hide, at least until they stopped looking hard for her. The other thing she realised today was that the world was small, anyone could see and recognise her.

Xena searched the Internet again for Daniel Dobrevski. Now that she knew what he looked like, maybe she would recognise him somewhere on the Internet. After an hour of searching, she gave up. She found nothing for this police inspector. Still, something about him bothered her. She didn't know what it was, but she would probably remember in time. She had a hard time falling asleep that night. She was tossing and turning in bed until late and when she finally fell asleep, she had nightmares.

In the morning, she made coffee and sat down on the armchair in the living room. She wouldn't be able to run today, the snow had accumulated and there was still no track. She had to spend the day at home. Xena exchanged a few words with her roommates, who were getting ready to go to work and stayed with her for a while to drink their coffee. Then everyone went out and there was silence in the room. She hadn't realised how lonely she felt until now. There was no one to call and just chat with. Dary was probably at work, but even if she wasn't, she didn't want to contact her and get her in trouble. Every night before she left for work, Xena heard her roommates talking carelessly with friends and relatives. They told them how their day went. Casual conversations she hadn't had in a long time. It was as if thunder had struck her this morning. She missed her old life, her friends, and her grandmother. She missed everyone. She was now caged and, like a bat, only came out at night. At least she was alive, she told herself and touched her neck again, the place where she had recently been strangled by two strong hands.

Xena spent the whole day at home drinking tea, making lunch and dinner. She realised she was worried about going out. The unwanted meeting had frightened her yesterday. Dobrevski had startled her and brought her back deep into reality. When it was finally time to go to work, she calmed down. She had made the best decision when she decided to look for a job at a nightclub.

There weren't many people in the club. She changed, exchanged a few words with some of her colleagues and her composure returned.

Several more winter months passed. Xena chose to work on all holidays, she had nowhere to go and no one to celebrate with. Gal was in the same situation. They got along very well. The young owner relied on her. If someone didn't come to work for some reason, the first person he called to take over the shift was Xena. He raised her salary after the second month, but that's not why she liked working at this nightclub. In fact, she liked working for Gal. His attitude towards people was humane. He once caught one of the bartenders stealing money from the till. He called the bartender aside, talked to him and they parted almost amicably. This bartender kept coming to help them sometimes when they had big events. Xena once asked him what Gal had said to him after he had caught him stealing. The answer was that they had talked about everything but that. Typical of Gal. If you didn't step on his feet hard, he would just move his legs, but if you stepped on his feet hard, the savage inside him would rise.

The way he dealt with drunken, impudent customers was strange. He endured all their insults and finally, in a calm voice asked them to pay their bills and leave. Gal had been born for this job. There were no fights at his nightclub, no complaints, and no one was rude to the staff. And the nightclub was full every night. Often on Friday and Saturday nights, a queue of people could be seen waiting to enter. The prices were not high, and the service was up to standard. The place was known for its secrecy and cozy atmosphere. Famous and scandalous people often came, but there was a separate entrance for them.

After the meeting with Dobrevski, Xena started to put on even more makeup. She lined her eyes with eyeliner and some of the clients thought she was Asian, though it didn't make sense because her eyes were blue. That suited her perfectly. The problem was that with this vision, she was attracting more attention than before. Her gait had become slightly springy as a result of karate training. Her body moved smoothly and flexibly and this attracted the eyes of men. The male clientele often tried to talk to her, gave her provocative looks or tried to get her a drink. Xena always refused them with a smile. Some of her colleagues tried to figure out how so many men liked her, but she didn't like any of them. She answered them with jokes and generally went out of context. She didn't care about men, a love affair would only distract her and that could put her in danger.

The other truth was that it was the kind of men who came to this nightclub that she didn't like. Of course, there were decent and nice customers, but she was sure they liked Xena the waitress, not the real Xena. She couldn't imagine any of them liking her after she took off her makeup. Makeup was her cover. Gal had once told her that he would have no problem if she came to work without that much makeup, that he wouldn't fire her. Gal's typical humor concealed the real reason for starting the conversation. She then told him that she felt safer that way and that the chances of a customer recognising her on the street were lower. Not that she was worried about working in a nightclub, she just didn't want guys in her life.

Xena thought her life seemed very simple, but it was complicated. She kept having nightmares and often woke up shouting. It took her two months to realise there was a problem with that. She knew she had to talk to someone. She was worried about going to a psychologist and she couldn't share with anyone what was pushing her into these nightmares. One of her roommates had experienced the loss of a parent and mentioned that she had talked to a friend and that helped her a lot. The other thing that helped her was to write the same phrase several times. It cleared her mind. Xena decided to try writing. It really helped her. Before she went to bed she wrote something and wrote it over and over again. Until she forgot what she was thinking before she started.

After a while Xena started drawing. She often made a figure with the pen and repeated it several times. Then she fell asleep and slept like a baby. It was as if the movement of the pen took the nightmares away. The kata also helped her during training. She wanted to have a bigger room and to be able to train at home, but for now she didn't want to move, although the salary she received and the tips her clients left her were enough for a flat. Xena, however, preferred to live with other people. This gave her peace of mind and she didn't feel alone all the time. The chatter of the people in the next room calmed her, though it sometimes made her sad.

Winter passed quickly, and spring returned beautiful and fragrant. Xena enjoyed the good weather, but when it rained and streams of water flowed into the canals, it reminded her of what had happened by the river a year ago. These days, she would go home and immerse herself in a movie or a book. She didn't want to think about what had happened then. Unfortunately, the memories came suddenly and the tears made their way. The trauma of what happened last spring spread throughout her body. Sometimes listening only to the rain outside, the sound of it made her shrink and get goosebumps. It made her feel wet and soaked from the river water as it was then, on the rock. The images were so clear that Xena began to shiver with cold even though the room was pleasantly warm. All this *deja vu* had a bad effect on her mentally. Each time she left, she looked around three times before leaving the front door. She looked at the reflections of people in the windows of cars and shops. It made her so tired that she ended up going to work tired. Eventually, Gal started to worry about her and made her go home and rest for a few days and return when she was ready.

She took his advice. Not that it helped, quite the opposite. Her stress worsened. Her lack of sleep caused shadows under her eyes. She had nervousness in her speech, her hands trembled, and worst of all, her heart began to skip beats. She could no longer eat, and had difficulty swallowing food so she ate mostly creamy foods. Xena had not eaten bread, fruits or vegetables for weeks. She didn't know how to handle it all. Pills and tea didn't help. She knew she had to relax and rest to regain her strength, but she didn't know how. The second day after he sent her home, Gal called her.

'Are you okay?' he asked.

'Not exactly,' she admitted. 'I can't rest and I hardly sleep.'

'I have an idea, but I don't know if you'll like it.' Xena didn't answer, but waited to hear the offer. 'I found you a man to talk to.'

'I can't involve anyone in this,' she said.

'And you don't have to. He has strange methods. He helped me. That's why I recommend him to you.'

Xena paused. She knew Gal had some problems, there were rumors, but it was the first time he'd talked about it.

'How long did it take you? I mean, get back to normal.'

'It's hard to say. Sometimes I still have fears and worries, but let's just say I can live with it now.'

'Give me a deadline so I know if I'm taking a chance,' she told him wearily.

'You can recover in two days, maybe in two weeks or months. Up to you.'

'Tell me about him.'

'Eccentric, I'm sure you'll like him. Look, Xena, I don't know what happened to you. I want to learn and what I know for sure is that you will not tell me, but you can trust me about this therapy. It worked for me, I sincerely hope it will help you too. There is nothing to lose. You are already a wreck.'

At the last sentence, Gal laughed. She knew he had said it just to challenge her and make her laugh.

'Okay, I'll trust you. What is required of me? What should I do?'

'I'll call and make an appointment with him. I hope he likes you. He doesn't work with people he doesn't like.'

'Okay. I hope I'm not sorry later or worse, you're sorry you got me into this.'

Although she couldn't see him, Xena was sure Gal was smiling slightly.

'I hear your smile,' she told him and smiled reluctantly.

'I'll call you later to tell you where and when to go,' he told her.

Late in the evening, Gal called her to tell her that there was an appointment for Dr. Baev the next day at ten in the morning.

'I was able to persuade him to see you as soon as possible. You owe me a drink,' Gal told her.

'I'll buy you a whole bottle,' she told him.

Xena did not want to go unprepared, she checked everything written about this doctor on the Internet and came across contradictory information about him.

She got up early in the morning and tried to get better. For the first time in days, she wore something other than pajamas. She looked in the mirror and the woman she saw there scared her. Pale, with dry lips, bruises under the eyes, and a tired look. She looked like a drug addict.

At exactly ten o'clock she stood in front of the office door and knocked. There was a slight cough from the office, as well as a claw-like sound on the floor. A dry male voice invited her inside.

Xena pressed the handle, opened the door and was surprised to find that a black dog's nose was pointed at her. A German Shepherd greeted her, sniffed her thoroughly, sniffed her bag then apparently lost interest and headed inside the office.

'You have to excuse Rurko, he has no particularly good manners. He thinks that our guests come here only to bring him treats. I hope you are not afraid of dogs.'

'Not at all,' Xena replied. 'On the contrary, I love them.'

The doctor nodded approvingly. He walked behind the desk and approached her. He held out a warm hand and introduced himself.

'Nice to see you in person, Xena. Gal talked to me about you for a long time and urged me to see you as soon as possible. Honestly, I see now that he was right to insist.'

Xena expected a question but he didn't ask her anything. The doctor turned his back on her and returned to his desk.

'What am I required to do? Do I have to answer any questions?'

'Not really,' said the doctor. He was slim and about fifty years old. His gaze was calm. He watched her openly with his gray-blue eyes. Later, she would think there was green in his eyes. She could not determine exactly what colour they were. Just like Dary's eyes.

'Okay, what do we do then?' she asked.

'We're going for a walk with the dog.'

'Right now?' Xena asked. Her anxiety immediately showed on her face.

'You're afraid to walk outside, aren't you?'

'You could say that,' she said.

'Okay, in that case, I'll go out and buy some sandwiches and you'll talk to Rurko.'

Xena's surprise was complete. She looked at the doctor puzzled. He was already putting on his spring coat and walking away to the door with an umbrella in his hand.

'You can leave if you don't want to wait for me but you'll miss the good food. So, you better stay. Rurko needs company. Right, boy?'

The dog answered with a short bark.

The doctor came out and Xena was left alone with the German Shepherd. The dog lay quietly in his bed, watching Xena with his beautiful brown eyes.

Xena stood in silence for a few minutes, then the dog came to her, sat at her feet and continued to look at her with the cutest look in the world.

'All right, Rurko. You want me to talk, right?'

The dog barked and returned to his previous position.

'Do you want me to tell you a story?' she asked him.

Rurko lay waiting. His eyes continued to follow her.

'All right. Let me tell you about my hometown Vedna. It is located high in the mountains and it is a divine place. Everywhere you turn there is greenery, but I like it best when the mountain is shrouded in fog. Then you can't see the peaks and you can only guess where the mountain ends and where the fog begins. It's magical. I have to take you there, you'll like it. I don't know if you will like the people, but nature, I'm sure you will fall in love with it and when I talked about people...'

Xena talked to the dog for almost an hour. Sometimes Rurko looked up in surprise and with a question in his eyes. To her surprise, he seemed to really understand what she was talking about. Sometimes he touched her with his paw. This dog was talented, he could listen. Intrigued by her story, Xena did not hear the doctor enter. She realised she wasn't alone when the dog stood up and ran to the doctor, burying his nose in the bag the doctor was holding.

'I see you two understand each other,' he said. 'Right? He knows how to keep quiet. That's why he's been with me for so many years.'

'How old is he?' Xena asked.

'He is nine years old. My friend is getting old fast and it only feels like yesterday when I took him in.'

The doctor looked at the dog with undisguised tenderness.

'I brought lunch,' he said at last and began to take the packaged food out of his bag.

'Some people don't like dogs,' he explained, 'and want normal therapy. In these cases, Rurko moves to sleep in the next room. He is not happy to be removed, but he is already used to it and sometimes as soon as the client enters the building he opens the door to the other room.'

Xena saw that there was a door on the left. The door was cleverly covered with a chair in front of it and if the doctor hadn't mentioned it, Xena wouldn't have paid attention. The food was delicious. She ate everything and began to clean up the remnants of the desk. Rurko had eaten his portion with only two bites and his eyes were now fixed on the remnants of the doctor's portion. It was as if he knew that some of it would be for him. When he finally received a few bites of meat, carefully separated from his owner especially for him, the dog lay down and visibly prepared to sleep.

'Rurko likes an afternoon nap. He sleeps for ten minutes, no more,' the doctor explained.

'I'm honestly surprised by your methods and your hospitality,' Xena said, pulling one of the portions toward her. She felt very comfortable in this office, as something cozy and warm.

'Most of my clients feel that way. Of course there are some who are disappointed.'

'I can't imagine anyone feeling uncomfortable here.'

'Well, Xena. Were you happy with your visit to us today?' he asked, now in a professional tone.

'Yes, I was very pleased.'

She smiled. For the first time in a long time she had eaten well. She felt calm and full. Her throat didn't tighten and she didn't want to cry.

'Do you want to come again in three days, on Friday?'

'Yes. I will be happy to come again.'

'I'll see you then. I'm afraid I can't give you more time. My friend Rurko and I need a short break.'

'Of course. Have a good day.'

Xena left the office with a pure heart. She didn't know what might have changed in a few hours, but she felt free and light. She went outside without looking around and decided to take a short walk. The rain had stopped and the spring sun was warm. She felt its warmth on her back. Xena walked on the streets without direction, without thinking about anything, wandered around window shopping, then sat on a bench in a small park and admired the blooming trees. It smelled like spring. The birds jumped from tree to tree and several bees attacked the blossoming apples and cherries in the park. It was idyllic. She hadn't felt that way in a long time. As a child, she had often gone to her grandmother's garden and sometimes drifted off by the heat of the sun and fell asleep on a bench by the wall of the house. She had loved those moments but she had forgotten about them. Gal was right, this eccentric knew how to help people like her. She would be grateful to Gal for life. She wrote him a thankyou text, he answered, *'I told you'* and a smiling emoticon almost immediately. Life was good, Xena told herself. She just needed to be reminded of it and maybe to get better she had to get a dog and talk to him. She laughed at the idea. Unfortunately, they didn't want dogs in the house where she lived. She herself hadn't wanted a dog until this morning. Now her opinion had changed.

Xena continued her life as before. The only change was her visit to the doctor. She always stayed alone with Rurko for about an hour until Dr. Baev came back with something for lunch. Xena talked to the dog and told him about her life and her worries. Sometimes she met his gaze and felt as if she were talking to a man. She revealed her soul to him and she knew he couldn't hurt her. He would not disappoint her. She hugged him sometimes, kissed his head, stroked his fluffy fur and he was happy about it. She learned to bring him dog treats and every time she entered Rurko's office he sat in front of her and waited impatiently for his treats. The doctor and his dog became a good part of her life. After only a month, she felt as close to them as to Dary and Gal. This strange therapy helped her and she happily made her way to the building where the doctor lived whenever she had an appointment.

Of course, Xena realised that she wasn't the only one using their services. She knew the doctor's hours were busy for the next three months and she was glad they had enough time for her. She always thought of them together, somehow, the dog and the doctor could not be separated in her mind. They were one. She couldn't even imagine the doctor's life without Rurko. Or vice versa. One day, she promised herself, she would get a dog and make it very happy. She would take very good care of it and she knew it would reciprocate. For now, however, she had to work and hide from many people.

Xena liked her job at the nightclub. She liked to go earlier and chat with her colleagues and Gal. She often went out of work with some of them. Her life had returned to normal. Until she saw him again.

The police inspector entered the nightclub and showed a picture to one of her colleagues. The moment she saw him, Xena walked behind the bar where Gal was standing and whispered to him, 'I have to go. I can't explain at the moment, maybe another time. Thank you for everything!'

The shocked Gal tried to grab her hand and stop her, but Xena pulled away quickly. She looked at him pleadingly and pointed to Dobrevski. Gal's gaze became tender and worried, but he said, 'Go. I will try to slow him down. Call me to let me know you're okay.'

Xena was already turning toward the back door, stopping long enough to nod to Gal and then sprinting out into the street. She was running again, he had found her again. She had to run, pack up quickly and go somewhere else.

When she approached the building where she lived, Xena saw the police. They had found her accommodation and not only were the police there, in one of the side streets Xena noticed one of Long One's men.

The blood ran from her face, and made her dizzy, but she regained equilibrium quickly, and turned and walked in the opposite direction. Her whole life was ruined again. She wondered how they had found her. Not that it mattered now, but whether someone had betrayed her. How did everyone suddenly show up?

Instinctively, Xena headed for the market. There were always a lot of people there, she could easily blend in with the crowd. Luckily for her, the market was full. She could hardly get away from people. The good weather had taken people outside even at this late hour. Xena found a place to eat and bought dinner.

Two hours later the market began to close for the night. She needed to find another place to stay. Or not. Maybe it was time to leave the country. Xena had been preparing for this stage of her life for a few months. Most of her money remained in her room but she still had enough to emigrate. She went to an Internet cafe and checked flights to London. There was one in four hours. Once she made the decision, the stress she had felt all day passed. She had to leave the country. She was not safe here anymore.

She could use Anna's ID and just disappear from here. She was likely to be caught, but decided to take a risk. She had nothing to lose.

Xena took a taxi to the airport. She bought a ticket and passed the customs check. She was worried all the time but she tried not to show it. Her plane would take off in an hour. She traveled without luggage, only with money and documents. However, no one was concerned about her. Just in case, she bought a few essentials from the shops at the airport while waiting for the exit to be announced.

5

NEW COUNTRY, NEW EXPERIENCE

Xena had never flown on a plane. She did not know what to expect and what would happen when she arrived in the United Kingdom, but she was relieved that no one knew her either. She would think about it later, now she just had to wait for the flight and take off. The airport was quickly filling with passengers. There were several other flights at the same time besides hers. People talked enthusiastically, while others stood and waited patiently on the benches. Xena walked around, she was nervous. Finally, everyone was called for her flight and she was amazed to see that at least a hundred people were heading for the gate. When she got on the plane she felt bad. The flight attendant saw her concern, approached her and asked, 'Is this your first flight?'

'Yes.'

'Don't worry, everything will be fine. Sit in your seat and relax. Press this button on top if you need something or want to talk to me.'

'Okay. Thank you,' Xena said and did as she was advised. A young couple sat next to her. The woman smiled at her and showed her how to fasten her belt.

'It's normal to worry the first time,' she said. 'You get used to it though after a few flights. The takeoff and landing can be a little unpleasant.'

Xena smiled nervously. Her stomach ached with anxiety not only from the flight, but from the unknown. All this reminded her of her escape by bus but now she was not going to a familiar place, but to a country unknown to her, with a different language and customs. She didn't know how to find a place to live or where to look for a job.

'Who are you going to in England? To relatives?' the woman next to her asked.

'No, I'm alone. I decided to try my luck there.'

'Well. You have to know that it's not easy in the beginning.'

'I know. I don't expect it to be easy.'

'Don't worry, when we land I'll show you the exit from the airport and where to catch the tube or train.'

'I'll be very grateful,' Xena said.

The plane creaked like an old car and began to move slowly on the runway. Xena grabbed the backrest. The woman next to her continued talking.

'We can help you with luggage too.'

'I don't have any luggage,' Xena said. 'I want to find a job and a place to live first and then my friends will send it to me.'

'You don't have any luggage?' the woman said.

'Only the essentials in my handbag,' Xena smiled nervously.

'You are very brave. Alone, without luggage. I would not dare to go alone.'

Xena thought that under normal circumstances she would not go alone, but said nothing. There was nothing normal about her life anymore.

The plane picked up speed and took off. Xena's ears were ringing. She tightened her grip on the backrests and expected it to be so throughout the flight. Only a few minutes later the plane reached altitude and there seemed to be silence. Xena heard people talking calmly, the flight attendants began handing out coffee, tea and water, as well as various foods. Xena didn't expect this, she thought she would be sick all the time, but her stomach calmed down and she rested her head on the backrest. She fell asleep for a while but awoke to the conversation of two young men behind her. One explained aloud to the other that they were staying with one person less in their house and now had to pay higher rent. The other was visibly dissatisfied, as he thought the rent had already been agreed in advance and there should be no change in the price. The argument lasted for a few minutes until they decided to quickly find someone else to live with them. Xena thought it could have been a great opportunity for her to find a place to stay quickly, but she didn't want to draw attention on the plane. Instead, she turned her attention to looking out the porthole.

A little later she fell asleep and dreamed that she was hiding outside again. Ivan was saying something to her and she couldn't hear him. It was as if he was warning her, making signs to her but she never understood what he wanted to say to her. She awoke with a slight cry. Fortunately, no one paid attention to her. She remembered that Ivan had died a long time ago and wondered why she was dreaming about him and what he wanted to tell her. Xena rested her head on the seat again. Most of the passengers on the plane were asleep, it was relatively quiet. The noise came only from the plane's engines. She hadn't imagined travelling by plane would be like that. She had always imagined that it was noisy and you could feel the speed. The couple next to her had also fallen asleep. How nice it would be to travel with someone else. To some extent, this seemed romantic to her. The two were huddled together, the man snoring slightly, but the woman obviously didn't mind. They slept peacefully and somehow carefree, like people who knew where they were going and what they were going to do. The complete opposite of her. Her life had turned upside down again but she would not give up. She had succeeded so far, she didn't believe it would get any worse.

A whisper came from the cabin crew. Then it was announced that the plane was starting to land. Xena watched the big city from the window and wondered what awaited her.

After landing, she approached the two young men who were talking about renting a room.

'I heard you have a room to rent. I'm looking for a place to stay and I was wondering if I could rent it.'

'Yes,' one of them said. He had a youthful smile but something in his eyes bothered her. 'It will be good for us too if you rent it.'

'Which part of London is it in? Can I come and take a look?'

'It's in North London. We're going straight to work now but tonight we can meet somewhere near the house and show it to you. I'm going to call the landlord to ask if they've found anyone. Wait for us after passport check, at the luggage area and we'll talk. Is that okay?'

'Yes, sure.'

Xena lined up in one of the queues to check the documents. She was worried that they would find out that her ID wasn't actually hers. Her hands were sweaty and her breathing was difficult. She hoped no one would see her concern. Fortunately, there was no problem. She and Anna were like twins, she was very lucky to find her ID card. The clerk at the counter showed her the way to the exit and she hurried there.

The airport was full of people of different nationalities. Xena paused for a moment because the new atmosphere stunned her slightly. All the signs were in English, most people spoke English and she realised now that she couldn't understand everything the people around her were saying. Xena panicked, not knowing where to go, as the signs around her said nothing. She had studied English for a long time but it was clearly not enough. Xena stood to the side so as not to disturb the crowd which was coming from everywhere and tried to calm down. She took a deep breath, closed her eyes briefly enough to get used to the noise and then opened them. Then she saw that, in fact, everyone was moving in one direction, so she followed the people.

Xena saw the boys in the baggage area, and headed for them.

'You're lucky,' said one of the boys, pulling her away from the people so they wouldn't hear them. 'The room is still vacant. However, the landlord wants a deposit for two weeks and rent for one month in advance. He won't let you in until he gets the money. The last roommate deceived him and he didn't want to take the risk again. He will come to our work to take the money.'

Xena pulled back slightly. She didn't want to rent a room without seeing it and give money like that, but she looked around and decided she had nothing to lose. She didn't know where to look for accommodation and this one appeared out of nowhere.

'How much are the rent and deposit?'

The amount they told her numbed her. That was almost all her money. She asked the boys to wait for her and went to the couple who were sitting next to her on the plane.

'Can you tell me how much the rent is for a room in London?'

The woman confirmed that this was the price in the slums.

'It's more expensive downtown,' they warned her.

Xena went to the toilet and counted out the amount requested. Only a few banknotes remained after paying the rent. She gave the boys the money, took their phone numbers and the address of the house. They agreed to call each other in the evening and meet somewhere.

Still restless and with a bad feeling, Xena left the airport and wandered off. She didn't know where to go. The man and woman from the plane found her that way, and helped her to buy a ticket to travel near the rented accommodation. She felt dizzy around so many people. The tube was narrow and noisy and the train was moving at the speed of an airplane. She travelled for about an hour and got off at the aforementioned stop.

Another shock followed her, the culture shock. People around her spoke all sorts of languages other than English. She didn't understand anything they said. Everyone walked very fast, pushed her and apologised. The streets were crowded with people in a hurry, there were not many wandering people like her. Fortunately, she heard a familiar language, approached the people who spoke her language and asked them where she could buy a SIM card. They guided her and continued their conversation. Luckily for her, the seller offered her a free SIM card. She loaded a few pounds onto it and calmed down. She now had a phone and could call the boys.

Xena began exploring the shops and the streets, drinking coffee at McDonald's and buying the cheapest sandwich possible. She asked for a job but everywhere they wanted documents she didn't have yet. One woman advised her to focus on cleaning houses while she got her paperwork done, which wasn't difficult, it just took time, two to three months. Xena started to worry. She had studied and was sure that she could work for the first three months without any problems, as she came from a European Union country, but it turned out that no one really wanted you if you didn't have a National Insurance Number. It would be harder than she thought, but at least she had a place to stay, she reassured herself.

When the meeting time came, Xena called Marin, as he had introduced himself. He didn't pick up. He didn't return the call and after her fifth attempt she was convinced that she had been deceived. Her hands began to tremble. She typed a text message just in case, telling them where she was and that she was waiting for them. After two hours of waiting, she was convinced that there would be no accommodation or money. The stress of the last few days affected her and she wept in the middle of the street. For a while no one paid attention to her, apparently people were used to such views. Only one woman approached and asked her if she was okay. Xena nodded, not daring to look the woman in the eye.

'Whatever makes you cry, don't worry,' the woman said. 'There were a lot of desperate people like you in this square who then prospered. Just don't think about it and keep going. Whether your boyfriend hurt you or you were fired, for whatever reason, go home and calm down.'

Xena said nothing and the woman left almost immediately in a hurry to do something urgent, probably. Xena sat for a while longer and didn't know where to go. She decided to go for a walk, not that she had a choice. She walked the streets for another hour or so, almost exhausted, then she sat on a bench. She looked ahead and saw the sign '*Hostel*'. Xena had heard that it was very cheap in hostels. You have to share a room with a few other people and sleep almost on the ground, but at least there is a bathroom and toilet. She looked at how much money she had and went into the hostel. She had enough to rent a bed for a week.

It was miserable inside, but it was still better than the street. There were people of different nationalities in her room. She

Deeply In The Soul

didn't know who to trust and who not to. Xena took the little luggage she had with her and went to the bathroom to take a shower. She tied a plastic bag over her things to keep them from getting wet and went into the shower with the bag. She had told herself on the plane that it couldn't be worse, but here she was, it turned out it could be worse. She was out of money and if she didn't find a job, she would soon be on the streets again, homeless. She had no clothes, except for the ones she had run away with.

Xena had the feeling that everything in front of her was collapsing. And how stupid she was. She was obviously a very easy target for the two young men. She remembered what she had said to the young family next to her. Apparently, the boys had heard her and taken advantage of it. A young woman not knowing anyone and for the first time on a plane, it is not far from logic to remember that just as she had heard their conversation, they had probably heard what she was saying. But it was too late to curse. A few months in a friendly environment had made her careless but that wouldn't happen again. Once she found a job and got back on her feet, she would make a plan B. One in which she would not leave all her money in her room and would not be found unprepared. She would learn lessons like this her whole life, she reminded herself. Not that she felt more educated now. On the contrary, she had never felt more stupid.

Xena was very tired, her eyes were closing, but she knew she would not be able to sleep peacefully that night. She wanted to lock herself in a safe place but instead she had to sleep in a room

107

with other people. The door to the room kept opening and closing all the time. After taking a shower, Xena sat up in her bed, put her bag with her belongings near the pillow and immediately fell asleep. She dreamt of Ivan again.

He called her, 'I told you.' He wanted to protect her, but a dead person couldn't protect her. Only living one could. Besides, if he had wished her well, she wouldn't have been where she was now and running away.

Xena slept restlessly, waking up often, shivering from the cold, even though the room was actually warm. She guessed she was shivering from the stress and tried to calm down. Xena imagined being with Rurko stroking his shiny fur. This helped; she fell asleep after a while and rested.

The hostel offered free tea and coffee every morning. She drank a cup of both, because she needed energy and went outside to look for work. She asked for jobs in cafes, restaurants, bars, and shops but without any documents, they didn't even want her as a cleaner. A woman advised her to look for the ads in the off licence stores. She told Xena that when she first came, she had found her first job there.

Xena found it difficult to speak English. She had studied a lot, but it was one thing to talk in front of a laptop, another to talk to people with different accents. She still managed, toured nearby shops, wrote a message on few ad boards, and then she returned to the hostel to rest for a while.

There was only one girl in the room when she got back. She smiled at her and Xena returned her smile.

'Are you looking for a job?' she asked in a strong accent.

'Yes, I'm looking for a job urgently.'

The girl handed her a business card. She seemed to find it difficult to speak English. In just a few words she explained to Xena that she had called an agency from this business card. They recruited cleaners without documents. The pay wasn't good, but at least it was a start.

'The work is hard,' the girl added.

'Thank you very much.' Xena hugged the girl. 'You're saving my life. My name is Anna and what is your name?'

'Lena.'

'Thank you, Lena.'

'A woman helped me two weeks ago,' Lena said. 'She gave me this business card. Now I give it to you.'

'Okay and I will give it to someone if they need it. I promise.'

Xena walked out of the hostel and rang the phone number on the card. A woman answered and asked her a few questions. Then she told her to go to their office the next day and texted her the address. Xena hoped to be hired. Even if the pay wasn't good, it would be better than nothing. Before she went to her room, she went to buy a sandwich for dinner. The girl at the hostel's reception told her that supermarkets have big discounts late in the evening on almost expired goods. She managed to buy a sandwich for only a few pence, which was her last. She would starve tomorrow. Xena hoped she would get hired and the starving would not last long.

She slept that night, got up early, feeling rested, but hungry. She tried to dull the hunger with a cup of tea and a cup of coffee then walked to the agency's office, knowing well that she didn't look good. She was clean but the clothes she wore hadn't been washed in days and were crumpled. She couldn't wash them because they wouldn't dry out quickly enough and she couldn't walk around the hostel naked. Xena only washed her underwear every night, squeezing it with a towel to dry it faster. This is what her grandmother used to do with her favourite clothes in the winter, when there was no heat and the clothes wouldn't dry for weeks.

Xena looked at her reflection in the window of the building, tried to smooth her T-shirt a little, and then finally decided to just button up her jacket to cover the folds.

The office was small, with three desks and a chair in front of each one. One of the women working there asked her to sit down and tell her about herself. She asked for her personal documents, phone number, email and address. Xena didn't know the hostel's address and didn't want to say she lived there. It would sound desperate. Instead, she wrote the address at which she should be living now. The woman on the other side of the desk nodded and wrote something down on the computer. There was an open packet of biscuits in front of her. The woman sipped her coffee from time to time and took a biscuit from the packet. It was torture for Xena to watch the woman's movements and claps. Hunger bothered her, but she said nothing and did nothing to show that she was hungry.

She stared intently at one point, waiting for the woman to finally start to talk about work and pay. However, nothing like that happened. After recording everything, she told Xena that she was free to go, and that she would be called tonight or tomorrow morning at the latest. Xena tried to ask something but the woman sipped her coffee and called for the next person.

The morning hadn't gone according to Xena's expectations. Now she didn't know if she was looking for a job or not. She hoped Lena would be in the room to tell her what was next, but she was gone. Her bed was made, the sheets changed, apparently Lena had left. Xena decided not to wait, but to keep looking for a job. She went to the shops to look at the new ads. She sent a few text messages and before sending the last one she received a message that there was no more money in the voucher and she had to top up. This brought her into deep reality. She had no money, no food and she didn't know if she had a job. There wasn't much money on her public transport card either, it would only be enough for one trip.

Xena went to a nearby park, sat on a bench, raised her knees and buried her head in them. She was cold, she wanted to cry, but she couldn't. Her tears were gone and she knew from experience that it wouldn't help her. She didn't know what to do, there was no way out of the situation she was in. Her only chance was to walk and pray for work and she did. She entered shops, restaurants and hotels but there was no success. Sometimes they took her phone number and promised to call her if they needed someone, other times they just sent her away. At the end of the day she was desperate.

Xena returned to the hostel without a job or food. She didn't even have the strength to take a shower, so she laid down on the bed and rested her head on the pillow. The question 'Why?' was spinning in her head with many variations to continue.

She looked around. There were new people in the room who looked as desperate as she did. Xena thought she hadn't reached the bottom yet, but if she didn't find work and food in a few days, she would join the Homeless shelter and that would be the bottom for her, worse than death.

Tears slowly flowed. Tears of helplessness and vulnerability. She feared that she would end up hungry and frozen on a street corner and the worst thing would be that no one would know who she really was. She had come in with a false identity and her life would simply disappear.

There is always worse, she thought. Her tears gradually stopped. No one knew that she was crying; her grief was quiet this time, silent. Xena lay down a little and then struggled to her feet. She tied her plastic bag again and went to take a shower.

In the shower, Xena wondered about good and bad, how intertwined they really were. How difficult it was to live only in good and only in bad. It was best for her to have balance. She had lost the balance and meaning of her life. She had run, and now she had nowhere left to run. Not that she had lost hope, but she had lost faith in people again.

No one called her in the evening and she was sure this was a sign that she would not be hired by the agency. She woke up hungry. She lay awake in bed late into the night, thinking about what she might do tomorrow.

When she woke it was very early in the morning and it was still dark outside. Her stomach churned, but she tried to ignore it. It was too early for free coffee and tea. She had to wait at least another hour. Xena tried to calculate how many more days she could stay in the hostel and realised that there weren't many.

She made a plan for the day, drank her free drinks and wandered around again looking for work. By noon she was tired. She had just decided to sit down and rest when her phone rang. One of the hotel managers was calling her. One of the cleaners hadn't come in to work today and he wanted Xena to replace her if she could. She would only work for six hours today. The pay wasn't much, but Xena jumped for joy. She walked to the hotel almost an hour early, for fear of his changing his mind. One of the maids reluctantly showed her what to do. She gave her work clothes and to Xena's relief she was able to disguise her miserable appearance. At the end of the day she was paid in cash, but there was no mention of whether she would be called again. But what had warmed her soul was the manager telling her, 'You did well for the first time.'

Xena looked at the money in her hand. She had to decide how to spend it so that it could help her survive for a few more days. She waited for the shops to discount their items and this time she bought bread and salad instead of a sandwich. If she was frugal, she could use this food for a few days. She bought a voucher for her phone, set aside a pound just in case and used the rest of the money to pay for another night at the hostel. Unfortunately, she had no money left for public transport.

Two more torturous days without work and money followed. The bread and salad were almost gone. Xena despaired again. On one of the quieter days at the hostel she managed to wash her jeans and T-shirt, putting them on one of the radiators in the hallway and wrapped herself in a large towel, which the lady at the front desk gave her for few hours.

Xena felt that she wouldn't be able to afford to stay here for a few more days. One of the boys at the hostel recommended that she go to a kitchen for poor people and sign up there for food. He gave her the address but Xena did not go. It was too far from the hostel.

She had been looking for work for two days, her legs no longer held her, her nerves were shot, but she tried not to show it to others. She dried her clothes and ate her last slice of bread. Her salad was spoiled and she had to throw it away. Her heart ached when she left it in the bin. Hunger was eating away at her, but more than anything, she was devastated by her growing anxiety. In the evening she looked in the mirror and hardly recognised herself. In just one week she had lost a lot of weight and she had blue circles around her eyes, but what bothered her the most were her own eyes, or rather her gaze. It looked desperate and vulnerable. She looked lost. What was happening to her was ruining her little by little.

Xena decided to get more sleep the next morning to regain at least some strength. She still kept the last pound and in the evening she would go and buy something to eat with it. Her life was not over yet, she told herself. It was just harder than expected but there was still hope. With that thought, Xena buried her head deep in the pillow and fell asleep.

She dreamed of him again. Ivan was talking to her. He told her, 'Wake up! Wake up! Wake up!' And Xena woke up. Her phone rang. The cleaning agency had a day job for her. They sent her the address she needed to go to immediately. Fortunately, it was not far from the hostel. Xena failed to take advantage of the free drinks that morning. Instead, she got ready as quickly as possible and walked to the address she had been given.

It turned out to be a hotel job again. She had to work eight hours and she would be paid in a week. Still good, she thought and she did her best. She even worked a half an hour extra to make a good impression on the manager. When she left, however, fatigue knocked her down. Xena sat down on the nearest bench and realised she had no strength to walk. She stayed there for half an hour and finally struggled to her feet and headed for one of the supermarkets. She bought herself bread only. She had to save and could not afford to buy anything else. Xena was so hungry that she began to eat the bread as she walked.

Finally, she returned to the hostel, took a quick hot shower and laid down in bed relieved. It struck her that the people in the room had changed again. She had remained the longest resident in this room over the course of the week. She relaxed in bed, no longer wondering who was coming in, who was leaving, she wasn't worried about security. Xena began to get used to the atmosphere and noise in the hostel. She no longer woke up at night waiting for someone to attack her. She had resigned herself to the place, and what could anyone want from her here? She had nothing. She had no money, no belongings, and even her food was scarce. She just slept. Fatigue permeated her whole body.

Xena woke up in the next morning from the nice smell of coffee. Someone had entered the room with a coffee in hand. Actually with a coffee maker. One of the girls looked at her and gestured to her if she wanted a cup of coffee too. She pointed to a clean cup and sugar. Xena agreed gratefully. She hadn't had real coffee in a long time. The coffee they offered at the hostel was not the best, even though it was free.

The girl poured the coffee into a cup and handed it to Xena. Xena wrapped her arms around the cup and inhaled the aroma almost happily. The girl laughed.

'Don't speak English,' she told her.

'No problem,' Xena said. Then added 'Thanks!'

Sitting in their beds, they both drank slowly from the warm liquid and enjoyed the drink.

'You made my day good,' Xena told the girl. She nodded that she understood.

Later, Xena took care of her morning outfit and when she returned to the room, the girl was gone. Xena really felt better this morning, with more strength and energy. She had eaten well last night and rested well, and her day had started well. She decided not to give up the free drinks today. After drinking them, she went to look for work. Unfortunately, Xena found nothing again. This was her last night at the hostel, if she didn't make any money by the next day at noon she would have to leave. She returned to the room for a moment, but decided to keep looking for job in the evening. She was worried about walking the streets alone at night but she would be out there for a long time tomorrow anyway; she had to get used to it.

Xena looked for work in a few nightclubs, explaining that she had experience. They listened to her, picked up her phone number and finally sent her away. By two in the morning she was in complete despair. A bar she went in after three o'clock was still open and fortunately she was hired there for a few hours. She had to clean the tables, and she was forbidden to enter behind the bar or in the warehouse. Xena stayed at work until morning and was paid enough to be able to rent a bed for another two days and buy more food.

She returned to the room very tired. She was just about to go to bed when her phone rang. The manager of the first hotel offered her a job during the day for six hours. Despite her fatigue, Xena agreed, and in just an hour, she cleaned the hotel rooms. She was happy to have a job that day. She could secure some more time with the money.

In the evening she returned with trembling knees. Out of fatigue, she didn't even feel like eating, but she knew she had to eat to be strong. And for the first time in a long time, Xena went to bed with a satisfied smile.

She worked day and night for the next few days. She was hired by the hotel for thirty hours a week and by the nightclub almost every night. Xena returned to the hostel every time exhausted, but she didn't complain. She managed to buy some clothes from a charity shop and could now change from time to time. She bathed twice a day to get rid of the smell of the nightclub and the sweat of working at the hotel. In both places, the work was hard but she held on. She had applied for documents and could not wait to be able to work legally.

After two weeks of hard work, Xena decided to take a day off and see if she could rent a place to stay. From the beginning of her stay in the UK, she realised that she would not be able to rent anything through an agency because she didn't have regular documents. Her only chance was to look for a room directly from the landlord. However, she was worried that she would be deceived again, so she had to postpone her search for a room to rent, but she didn't want to stay in the hostel either. Xena needed solitude and peace. She needed more money, of course, but she still wanted to gather information and have a plan. She visited several rooms for rent, which she discovered on the Internet. The conditions were more than good, but the rent was very high. She couldn't afford the rent and deposit. At the end of the day she gave up, she returned to the hostel and paid for a bed for another week.

The next week, Xena worked in both places again. The nightclub began to give her more responsibilities. She no longer only cleaned the tables but also arranged the goods in the warehouse. They extended her working hours by another two hours. She now worked for sixteen hours straight: eight hours during the day and eight hours at night. Every day, Xena would return to the hostel long enough to take a shower and fall asleep almost immediately. She hardly ate, not because she had no food, but because she had no time. She often bought a sandwich and ate it on her way to work. At the end of the week she took a day off from the hotel. She already had enough money to rent a room. The agency had paid her the promised wage for six hours. They had found her another job, but she refused. For now, she was fine at the hotel and the nightclub.

On her day off, Xena slept late. She needed to recharge her baterries. Then she did something she hadn't done in a long time, she wandered the streets without searching for anything, and sat down to drink coffee in the cafe. Coffee was expensive but it was good and gave her great pleasure. After that, she started looking for accommodation again. Luckily for her, there were a few places available. There was one room very small but cozy. The rent was not very high, but most of all she liked the people in the house. She had the feeling that they were good people. Xena took a risk and paid the deposit and rent. They signed a contract and at the end of the day, she moved in. Xena was so happy that the moment she lay down on the new and clean bed, she began to laugh out loud with joy. Fortunately, everyone in the house was downstairs and no one heard her. The room wasn't well furnished, but Xena didn't need much. She needed sheets and some utensils, but she would buy them in the next few days.

Xena's intuition about the people in her new place was right. Everyone was trying to help her in one way or another. They told her where she could shop cheaply, and gave her advice. None of them asked her who she was or where she was from. They just helped her without asking unnecessary questions. The people in the house were from different countries, and followed different religions. Nevertheless, peace and quiet reigned in the house.

Busy with two jobs, her days passed quickly and soon interview for her legal documents came. Xena left an hour early to make sure she was on time. Fifteen minutes after her appointment, the guards called her and directed her to one of the officers.

'Good afternoon,' Xena said.

'Good afternoon,' the man answered her.

Xena waited, and so did the man.

'You've made an appointment, but I can't understand why,' the man began. 'You already have a National Insurance Number.'

Xena tried to hide her surprise. Then she answered sensibly.

'That's right, but unfortunately I lost it and I want to ask if you can give me a copy.'

'I can give you a copy, but why didn't you ask for it online? You wouldn't have had to wait as long.'

'I tried, but I didn't succeed, so I decided to come straight here,' Xena lied, adding, 'I'm not good at new technology.'

'Yes, I understand,' the man smiled. 'It's not just you, a lot of people can't get used to it. They want to replace us with the Internet.'

Apparently this was something that worried him, because he went onto explain in detail to Xena how soon there would be no one in this office and how computers would replace everyone. After a ten-minute conversation, Xena got Anna's insurance number. Her heart sank. She was taking advantage of this woman's identity. She was ashamed of her actions but promised to find a way to regain her identity. She had to check on how to legally become a resident here with her real name, but now was not the time to think about it.

Xena spent several weeks at work without taking a break. She barely saw her roommates. They, like her, worked in two places, but mostly during the day, only she worked at night. When she finally decided to rest, she spent her day shopping. She sat down at Costa and drank their good coffee. Xena looked around at the people around her, some were happy, others worried. There was a colourful palette of different nationalities. She heard speech in languages that she didn't even know existed. Of course, she sometimes heard conversations in her mother language. Then she remembered her childhood, Dary and Gal. She had to write to them and tell them she was fine. Xena saw an internet cafe on one of the streets, and paid for an hour. Then she sent a message to Gal and Dary.

Xena missed them very much. She missed talking to Gal. She also missed the doctor and Rurko. Nostalgia overwhelmed her.

She hadn't had time to think about it before. She had been so absorbed in the search for work and the need for documents and accommodation. She had blunted the feeling of her lack of friends. Now she walked the streets alone, with no one to talk to and no one knew who she really was. In the hotel where she worked, she cleaned by herself, rarely talked to anyone, in the nightclub it was the same. People weren't worried about her or her feelings. Everyone was absorbed in their own problems and didn't want to burden themselves with strangers. Xena sent emails to her friends and sent one to the doctor too. Almost immediately she received an answer from Gal:

'I miss you, girl. Conquer the world and come back to me.'

Typical of Gal. He believed in her even when she didn't believe in herself. She was doing well, it was true, but not because she was ambitious, but because she had no choice. She had to eat and sleep somewhere. She didn't know if she would be as strong in other circumstances. Xena would certainly feel better if she had a stable man by her side. Her problem was that she no longer trusted men. For her, every man would think he owned her and would sell her to whomever he wanted. This feeling would probably never leave her and would probably prevent her from starting a new love affair. Xena wasn't looking for love now, though she knew love was a good thing. Right now, she needed independence and promised herself she would work hard to one day feel financially secure and that would make her free.

For the next month, Xena continued to work her two jobs. The nightclub increased her salary after she gave them her insurance number. Unfortunaly, the hotel only registered it, but her salary there remained the same.

Celebrations parties were often held in the nightclub and during the day, and the manager invited Xena to take part in the events a few times. After a while, Xena accepted. The pay was better than the hotel and the work much easier. She could now afford to choose where to work. The parties at the club took place at noon or in the afternoon, allowing Xena to sleep more in the morning. She gradually regained her good body, sometimes jogging early. She ran in the park and this had a good effect on her, not only on her body but also mentally. She was happier and full of life.

Her days and nights passed quickly, she continued to study English and took free courses once a week. There she met many people from different countries and realised how wrong her ideas about different nationalities were. The clichés in books and on the Internet were now being shattered by her new friends on the course. This course was her social life. The meetings and conversations with the people there calmed her down. They all seemed to understand her and help her understand British laws and customs. It turned out that almost everyone had similar problems to hers, and sharing with them proved to be good therapy. People often think that their lives are miserable and difficult, but when they meet people with the same problems, they realise that they are not alone. And this thought somehow calmed them. Xena felt the same way. It was as if she was no longer alone.

One autumn day, the nightclub manager offered her a job to go with her and two other girls to a party in South England. They would travel for more than seven hours, organise the party and return. That meant almost two days without a break. The hotel where the event was to be held was on the oceanfront, in a small resort in Cornwall. Xena accepted with pleasure and was very excited. She had never seen the sea or the ocean. Born and raised in a mountain town, she dreamed of going on vacation to the sea but never managed to do it. Now she would finally hear the sound of the waves. Although she had to work, Xena was sure she would be able to get to the beach for at least five minutes.

Their trip took almost eight hours. They arrived just in time to start organising the party. The hotel restaurant overlooked the ocean and Xena stared outside in amazement. The waves were high and many surfers had boarded and attacked them. They looked like little black ants from where Xena was looking at them. Sea foam remained on the shore and the dogs played with it. The air was fresh, the people around were calm and smiling. Cornwall had nothing to do with London. The beauty of this place impressed her. Not just the ocean, everything here was impressive and somehow reassuring. Xena decided to do her best to get a better look at this beautiful part of the world, but before that they had to prepare the party. Four women had come from London and two other girls were helping them from the local town. However, the decoration, preparation of the bar and menu took almost the whole day. The party was late and the first guests were expected at eight in the evening. At half past seven, everything was ready and the staff was in place. Xena had to work as an assistant bartender. She liked that. She'd rather be behind the bar than be a waitress and listen to drunken guests. She learned from her boss that a large part of Britain's political elite would be present at the party. For this reason, all their phones were confiscated and they signed a confidentiality agreement. Everything that happened at the party had to stay there. No photos and recordings.

Shortly after eight in the evening the guests began to arrive. Xena was unfamiliar with British politicians, and didn't recognise anyone, but the head bartender, himself a famous person, kept her informed of anyone who arrived and sometimes supplemented the information with some juicy gossip Xena was not one of those people who cared about the private lives of politicians. Who was she to judge them? The bartender would be amazed at how strange her life was and how far she had come. So Xena nodded at everything he shared with her and smiled slightly if he told her anything interesting about people taking drinks from them.

The party lasted until late. Many of the men and some of the women got drunk, some of the guests didn't seem to be just drinking, but Xena tried not to think about it. She didn't want to interfere with anything illegal, so she didn't question her famous colleague. While the alcohol was almost gone, the food on the tables remained almost intact. These people were not hungry, they were just thirsty. Xena thought she could have fed a small village with the food, but she knew that at the end of the party, all these delicious sandwiches and delicacies would end up in a black rubbish bag and even the animals would not get to taste it. The food would be thrown out without a problem or remorse by any of those present at the party.

By the end of the party, only a few guests remained and Xena saw a chance to go ashore and take a walk in the fresh air. Her boss and bartender gave her half an hour off. Xena came out, inhaled the sea air and stared into the darkness in front of her. She could hear the sound of the waves crashing against the shore and spilling over the sand. She could feel the strong energy of the elements. The wind ruffled her hair, but she didn't worry, she'd fix it after the walk. Xena started walking along the shore. She walked slowly, the lights of the hotel allowing her to see most of the bay. There were no boats here, but in the distance she could see the lights of a ship moving slowly and heading west.

Other people, probably guests of the hotel, were walking around her. Most were couples, some visibly in love, holding hands, others engaged in calm conversation or argument. There were almost no singles like her. Xena decided not to go too far, as she did not have much time. She took off her shoes and walked barefoot into the cold water. Sea foam wrapped around her legs. The small bubbles burst as she stepped on them. Despite the cold water, Xena felt calm. It was like water therapy, pulling back and then wrapping her feet again. Her footsteps stayed for a moment, then the water washed them away.

Time passed quickly and Xena regretfully decided that she had to return to work. She tried to clean her feet as best as she could, put on her formal shoes and returned to the party which was now over.

The staff picked up everything from the tables. Xena helped the bartender arrange the drinks and wash the glasses, then joined in to help everyone else. At seven o'clock in the morning, the four women got in the car and headed back to London. Two of them fell asleep almost immediately, but Xena and her boss stayed awake. Her boss was driving and Xena dreamed of returning to this paradise place and learning to surf, and to ride the waves. She was very impressed by the nature of this small town. Unlike the bartender, who was proud to serve all these prominent politicians and their friends, Xena was impressed not by the people but by the place. She promised herself to come back one day and take a walk along the coast.

'Why aren't you sleeping?' her boss asked her.

'I was thinking about Cornwall,' Xena said.

'You liked it there, didn't you?'

'A lot. I would like to go back again and learn to surf.'

'Next month there is another party there that we have to prepare. I will try to book a hotel for then and stay one day to rest. I'll take you around. I was born in Cornwall and I miss this place so much.'

'That would be great,' Xena said enthusiastically. She looked at her boss and saw her with different eyes. Lisa was a little older than Xena. She was strict, but she was fair to her staff. So far, she had only a strictly professional relationship with Xena and she realised that she knew nothing about her. Neither where she lived, nor with whom. Her boss kept her personal life away from work as Xena did. When someone asked her where she lived and with whom, she answered evasively.

Xena had learned from her mistakes. She was convinced that someone at Gal's bar had revealed where she lived. She would not repeat that mistake in London. The nightclub she worked at didn't provide staff transportation, as Gal did. They usually finished work when the tube started to run again and Xena used public transport, always getting off at a different stop. Then she would get on a bus or just walk. The morning air refreshed her. She hid where she lived from everyone, she also hid where she worked from her roommates. She told them she worked for a chain of nightclubs and was sent to a different place every week. Not that she saw the people she lived with often. They worked during the day, she at night and often they just passed each other at the front door.

Xena's thoughts turned to Cornwall again. She had always thought the sea in the bays were calm. She was obviously wrong, but how would she feel looking at a calm sea? The view would probably be amazing.

Xena imagined drinking her coffee at an ocean front bar and watching the waves. There was something magical about this place, something that made her want to go back there. She couldn't imagine why her boss preferred London to Cornwall, but she probably had no choice. Or she had run away from something, just like Xena.

Xena had never imagined herself as an immigrant. If she hadn't had to, she would probably never have left her country. Now almost settled in a new country, she realised that the people and nature in the two countries were very similar. Also, in both countries there were hungry people and there were some who were full. The myth that money just rains when you move to London had collapsed for her in the first few hours, but the strange thing was that she liked living here. She met different people, with different religions and beliefs. Xena was interested when they told her about the countries and places they came from. Sometimes intrigued, she searched the Internet for more information about the country, which in some cases, she hadn't even heard of it. For example, the country of Eritrea. She didn't know about the wars, she didn't know about the people there, until she met the woman who was cleaning the bar in the evening. A beautiful intelligent young woman, who came to live with her husband in London three years ago. A wonderful young family with a difficult history behind them. Nothing was just black and white in London. Everything went gray. Xena realised that although she didn't think so at first, she was actually lucky and strange as it may have been, things had happened to her quickly and briefly. Some people were in the difficult situation of not having food and money, or a secure roof over their heads for years and since some of them were still in the country illegally. Their agony would continue for a very long time.

'Can you swim?' Lisa interrupted her thoughts.

'I can,' Xena smiled.

'Then next time we'll take our swimsuits and I will give you a surfing lesson.'

'I can't wait.' Xena's smile widened.

Their journey was almost over. They entered the motorway traffic and Lisa focused on driving. An hour later, everyone was home, exhausted from the two-day trip and work and fell into a deep sleep. Not Xena. It took her another hour to dream of climbing a wave made by the ocean. Then she slept soundly and woke up after almost ten hours. She woke up from the ring on her phone. The cleaning agency wanted her to work for them. Xena refused politely and continued to sleep for another hour and a half. She hadn't slept that long since she was a child. Her sleep worked well. She felt new and refreshed not only physically but mentally. She already had a place to look and something to dream about. After a short stay, she got up and prepared to go to work again. Her life was returning back to everyday life.

For a few months, Xena worked at the bar and nothing interesting happened in her life. The nightclub was mostly filled with young people. They had the most work on Friday night, that's why all the staff gathered then. In fact, there were two bars and customers could choose which bar to buy drinks from. No food was offered, not even nuts and crisps, which was strange to Xena, but the traditions here were different.

She worked as an assistant bartender most evenings. People often talked to her and when they heard her accent, began to ask her where she came from and whether she liked London. She answered briefly and always steered the conversation in another direction. Some of the bar's customers came to her especially, they felt special when she spoke to them and remembered their names. She had learned to add a name to the face since Gal's nightclub. He had trained her to recognise customers who were coming for the first time and to give special treatment to customers who were already coming. Gal knew how to caress people's egos, even hers. She used this tactic here as well and soon became famous in the neighbourhood.

When Xena was off, some customers didn't come and the owner of the club was dissatisfied. He wanted her to work every night. However, Lisa always stood up for Xena and even insisted that her salary should be raised by forty percent. After about a month, the owner of the nightclub agreed. His competition had shown great interest in his beautiful bartender and he was worried she would leave. Xena didn't know why her customers liked her so much. She treated them no differently than her clients in her hometown and at Gal's club. The fact was, that in just a few months she became very popular and she began to worry about that. She didn't want to be seen because someone could recognise her. On the other hand, her pay was more than good and she didn't want to leave.

Xena's roommates changed in those months, and now she lived with three boys and a girl. One of the boys and the girl were a couple. They didn't have to say they loved each other. It was visible from afar and for Xena it was a reminder that she had been alone for a long time. She had no friends, she didn't share with anyone.

Sometimes she stopped at an Internet cafe and exchanged a few emails with Gal and Dary. She missed them very much. She also missed Ivan, she sometimes mentally talked to him. As she missed Adi and her grandmother. Xena wondered what Adi was doing. Did she still think she had killed Ivan? It was hard to find out what was going on. She had had no contact with anyone from Vedna and there was no new information on the Internet about Ivan's murder. Her old life seemed distant and didn't seem like it was her, but someone else. Sometimes she imagined that none of this had happened and that she would wake up, put on her torn trainers and run to the stadium. Then she would meet Ivan and as always, she would find solace in him. But Xena didn't wake up. The reality was different, the past was there and although she lived under a different identity, it was clear to her that one day her past would catch up with her. It only reassured her that this day was not today and it was not now. She learned from Gal that Dobrevski was still looking for her. Gal, like Dary, thought Xena should contact this man and talk to him.

'Nothing in it says he is against you, Xena,' the young man had written to her. 'He wants to help you, not hurt you,' but Xena didn't trust the police and institutions. The presence of Long

One's men in front of her apartment clearly showed her that the moment the police knew where she was, Long One's people knew she was there too. Therefore, she thought it was better to stay away and in a safe place. The only thing that bothered her was that, according to Gal, Dobrevski already knew that Xena was in London. So Xena began to consider leaving London and she liked the idea of moving to Cornwall more and more every day. There was only one problem, she needed a bank account, which she had delayed opening for months. The nightclub still paid her in cash, but that would be over soon. Xena knew that if she opened a bank account everyone would have her address. The other problem was that the ID card with which she introduced herself as Anna expired in a few months and she would soon be unable to use it unless she went to the Bulgarian embassy and submitted a request for renewal. The problem came from the fact that the real Anna had probably already renewed it, so they would catch Xena with her documents.

For now, however, Xena didn't want to think about it. She took a two-week break from such thoughts and focused on training in the morning and working in the evening. She wanted to be physically fit again, so she started attending a karate club twice a week. Fortunately, no one there asked her who she was. She paid in cash and trained with about twenty other people. Each time she came home exhausted but mentally calm. Karate helped her relax. She learned two more short Kata, which she sometimes practiced at home. Ever since Gal wrote to her that Dobrevski knew she was in London, Xena had stopped running in the morning. She was worried that someone might meet her by chance. It turned out that the world was small and she could easily come across someone familiar.

A month later, Xena made an appointment at the embassy to change Anna'a ID card. She had to fill in an online declaration with the card details and indicate her address in London. She rewrote the address the boys from the plane had given her. She didn't want to take any chances and yet something disturbed her as she filled out all the data. That same day, her boss informed her that they were leaving for Cornwall the next day, this time for three days. This fixed Xena's bad mood. She packed her bags as quickly as possible because they had to travel as soon as they finished work at the nightclub.

Xena, Lisa and another of the girls left in the dark. This time the way Lisa chose was calmer. They passed Stonehenge and Lisa briefly told her the story of the place. The strange thing for Xena was that sheep were grazing around the tall stone blocks. The sight was somewhat reassuring. They passed through Somerset and Devon and were in Cornwall early in the morning.

The party they had to prepare was in the same hotel and the staff would be almost the same. The preparation itself didn't take long, everyone already knew where to stand. The only problem was that the famous bartender had been stuck in traffic for few hours and the chance of arriving on time was minimal. Xena had to take over his business and Lisa had to help her as much as she could.

Xena wasn't worried. She knew how to pour drinks and talk to guests. She managed to do well until the bartender came and as a thank you, the party organiser gave her a good tip.

'Everyone likes you,' Lisa told her. 'You could easily become a famous bartender.'

'I have no such ambitions,' Xena said. 'I still have no intention of leaving the nightclub.'

Lisa nodded and smiled contentedly. She did't want to part with her best worker. Xena was all a nightclub boss needed. She worked long hours without getting tired, she could talk to clients and not judge them and they all liked her very much. Naturally, the men flocked like bees to honey but Xena didn't seem phased by the attention, and she wasn't too friendly with them either. Some customers had suggested that Xena was gay, but after unsuccessful attempts at flirting by the female sex, everyone decided she had a boyfriend, but didn't want to show it off.

However, Lisa was sure that there was no partner in Xena's life. Sometimes, when she thought she was alone, Lisa would catch her looking alone. This girl was definitely unattached, something was keeping her from getting engaged.

The party went very well. Xena and Lisa went back to their hotel and arranged to see each other at noon. Xena didn't want to waste so much time, she wanted to walk along the shore and look around, but Lisa was tired and needed sleep.

After the rest, the two women had lunch and a cup of coffee, then rented wetsuits and a surfboard and dived into the ocean. For a few hours, Lisa showed Xena how to stay on the board for as long as possible. Finally, after several unsuccessful attempts, Xena briefly managed to catch a wave. She smiled happily and kept trying. After another hour of playing with the waves, she came out of the water and lay happily tired on the sand. Two dogs automatically came to check if she was okay and started licking her face. She had never felt so free and happy.

'Did you like it?' Lisa asked her.

'A lot, I haven't done anything so crazy before,' Xena said.

'I see you're having a lot of fun. Do you have the strength to walk?'

'Yes,' Xena said with twinkling eyes. She felt in great shape.

Lisa suggested they go change and advised her to wear something warmer. Half an hour later, the two of them were walking along the shoreline. The ocean was turquoise. Seagulls and other birds made their sounds, but for Xena in general, everything around her brought some reassurance. As if nothing else mattered, only this moment and this sight. She looked at the landscape around her, took a few photos and just when she thought she wouldn't see a better view, she saw a few seals resting. It was an amazing experience, she didn't even know there were seals in Cornwall. Their walk lasted a long time, they walked along the coast, passed through several small towns and finally stopped in front of a restaurant. The restaurant had access to the sea, with a beautiful view which could be seen from the shore with many customers. The moment they entered, Xena realised that this was no accident they are there. Everyone greeted and hugged Lisa, telling her they were glad to see her. To the question in her eyes, Lisa answered.

'I grew up here. This is our family restaurant,' then Xena was introduced to her mother, father and brothers.

'I didn't mean to intrude,' Xena said, realising that everyone greeted her as a guest of honor.

'You're not intruding. I see how much you like everything here and I wanted to show you around. Now you will eat the most delicious fish and chips in the whole area.'

Lisa's family prepared a table for them and brought them drinks. People kept coming and talking to Lisa and sometimes including Xena in the conversation. Xena was left with the impression that she had met the whole family, as well as all the friends and acquaintances of her boss. When they were finally left alone for a few minutes, Xena asked her, 'Why did you leave all this?'

'I don't know, to be honest. Now that I'm here, I'm wondering why,' Lisa smiled.

'You have a wonderful family.'

'Thanks! Be careful with my brothers, one has already decided that you are his mermaid.'

Xena laughed out loud. She had been called some things, but it was the first time she had been called a mermaid.

Xena became infected with the pleasant atmosphere and company, and relaxed like never before. She ate a double portion of fish and chips. As Lisa had promised, they were the best she had ever eaten. After dinner and the restaurant closed, everyone moved to the beach. They lit a small fire, took the beer and soft drinks and relaxed in conversation. Xena met these people a few hours ago but she already felt like she had known them for years. Lisa had walked away briefly with one of her friends. Xena looked at them and had the feeling that they were arguing about something.

'That's her ex Dylan,' said Ryan, Lisa's little brother. 'He dumped her for another girl and now he's convincing her he's wrong.'

'Your sister is a wonderful person. Dylan made a big mistake of dumping her.'

'We think so too and he's obviously realised his mistake. She left because of him. She didn't want to see him, but as you can see, the moment he saw her, he couldn't leave her alone.'

Xena now understood why Lisa had left. Apparently everything reminded her of her ex and his infidelity.

'If I meet such a woman, I will never do such a thing to her,' Ryan continued, looking at Xena meaningfully.

She pretended not to understand the hint. She liked Lisa's family and didn't want to cause trouble, and embark on love adventures.

Lisa approached them and said, 'Don't believe a word Ryan says to you. He is known for courting beautiful women.'

'And that was my sister.' Ryan smiled broadly and hugged his sister. 'I only compliment the best women.'

He looked at Xena meaningfully again, but she looked away. She felt awkward. She stared at the ocean and the waves lapping at the beach. Ryan and she lived on two different planets, that was for sure, there was no way to get between them.

At almost midnight, Ryan drove them back to the hotel, inviting Xena to visit them as soon as possible. Xena smiled gently and politely accepted the invitation.

'Bring the mermaid again,' he whispered to his sister, but loud enough for Xena to hear him.

'Of course. Good night, brother,' said Lisa.

The two women went back to their rooms, each taking their thoughts from the day. Xena lay down and smiled broadly. The world wasn't so bad, she thought. Some people really enjoyed life. She fell asleep late and felt very tired in the morning. Lisa also looked tired.

'I couldn't sleep until late last night,' she told her.

'Me too,' Xena said.

They had breakfast, two cups of coffee and headed back to London.

'You have a wonderful family,' Xena said.

'That's right. My parents are good people. I had a happy childhood. And you? Do you have a family? Do you miss them?'

'I'm alone. My grandmother raised me, but she died a few years ago.'

'And a boyfriend or girlfriend?'

'I had both. Unfortunately we lost contact some time ago.'

'Maybe you should go see them someday,' Lisa suggested.

'Maybe.'

Xena didn't want to tell her story, so she just tilted her head back and ended the conversation. Lisa gave her a questioning look, but Xena pretended not to see her and was getting ready to sleep. The trip was long and as they travelled during the day there was traffic. It took them almost a day to return to London.

Xena thanked Lisa warmly for a wonderful day at the beach and with her family and returned home tired. Her back and lower back ached from the trip. There was no time to rest, she had to go to work in the nightclub in two hours, so she opened her laptop. She had received emails from Gal and Dary. Dary was engaged and expecting a baby. The news made Xena smile broadly. At least one person close to her was happy. However, Gal was worried about Xena. He wanted to come to London and see her. He ignored the fact that someone could track him down and find her very quickly. So Xena turned down his offer. She hoped that one day she would be able to see and talk to her friends calmly, without fear for her and their lives. Gal's email brought her back to reality. She had to try to renew her documents, otherwise her life would become more difficult. A month later, she had an appointment at the embassy and she hoped everything would go well.

The month passed very quickly. Xena's days were the same from work to home, and from home to work. The nightclub was busy, and she was less and less able to take a break. Xena felt tired, even skipping two karate practices so she could sleep for a few more hours. She didn't usually get tired so quickly, she was resilient, but she hadn't slept properly for almost a week. She was nervous and worried, there were dark circles under her eyes and this didn't go unnoticed by Lisa and her colleagues.

'Do you have problems?' her boss asked her.

'No. Why do you ask?'

'You don't look like yourself. Tell me if you need a day off.'

'No, don't worry. I've just been having a hard time falling asleep lately.'

Lisa nodded. She hadn't been able to sleep on her own since they came back from Cornwall. She hadn't imagined that she missed her family and friends so much until she saw them. Now she was faced with the dilemma of whether to return there or stay in London.

Xena had a more difficult dilemma, to go to the Bulgarian Embassy or not. Her intuition told her not to go, but the owner of the club insisted on paying her by bank transfer and she needed the new documents. Moreover, no bank would open a bank account with an ID card alone; she needed a passport. After long sleepless hours, on the day she was due at the Embassy, Xena decided to take a chance. She went earlier to inspect the building and to see if anyone was waiting for her. She wandered around for almost half an hour, looking around and seeing nothing suspicious. Ten minutes before the scheduled time, Xena entered the embassy building and saw him immediately. Their eyes met, she started to turn and leave, but the guards stopped her. Dobrevski brought her closer.

'Don't run, I just want to talk with you,' he reassured her. His eyes were dark brown, worried. There were a few green, barely visible glints just around his pupils, which added extra softness. Xena stared at him and told herself not to worry, but the presence of the guards behind her quickly returned her fear. They probably wanted to arrest her, but they didn't want to do it in front of all those people who were in the room right now.

'All right,' Xena's voice trembled slightly. Her anxiety was visible. She didn't know what came next.

'Come here, the embassy staff gave me a room for about half an hour. If we don't reach a decision by then, you will be free to leave.'

Xena looked at him in disbelief. She had used other people's IDs, they would hardly let her go. She decided she had no choice and followed the man. She felt her knees weaken and her hands tremble.

'Do you want something to drink?' he asked her.

'No,' she said shortly.

'I'll pour you some water at least, it can help you calm down.' Dobrevski looked meaningfully at her hands.

'Okay, I'll have a glass of water,' Xena said, sitting in the empty chair in front of her. She expected to be interrogated for an hour, a little water would not hurt her.

Dobrevski poured water from a jug into two glasses. He placed one glass in front of her, the other on his right. Xena thought he was probably right-handed. She didn't know why this thought came to her, she looked away from him and focused on the glass in front of her. She took a sip of water and looked at the man on the other side of the desk. Only now did she notice that there was another person in the room. He was about fifty years old, with a military stance. His eyes were brown, his eyebrows thick and lush and his gaze stern. If Dobrevski had calmed her down a few seconds ago, Xena was worried again. The older man in the room scared her a lot.

'Don't worry,' Dobrevski followed her gaze. 'That's how he looks, he looks scary but he is ok. This is Inspector Ivanov. You are not in danger, you have not done anything wrong, we just want to talk to you about the circumstances surrounding the death of your boyfriend Ivan.'

Xena looked away from Ivanov and nodded slightly.

'Will you tell us what happened the day he was killed?' Dobrevski asked and smiled reassuringly at her.

'I know he was killed, but I don't know exactly which day,' Xena said. 'I only know what was written on the Internet.'

'He was killed late at night after you met him. According to reports from his phone, you had a meeting at the upper end of the river.'

Xena nodded, memories flooding in. She swallows loudly, her mouth gets dry.

'So, he was killed that night?' Xena asked.

'Yes.'

Xena swallowed loudly again and, surprisingly for her and the men against her, tears welled up in her eyes. The emotions of that distant spring day flooded her.

'Drink water. It can help you calm down,' Dobrevski suggested again.

Xena wiped her tears with her hand, drank some of the water and it really calmed her down. The two men said nothing, waiting for her to start talking.

Xena told them what had happened briefly, but they began to ask questions and made her recall details she thought she had forgotten. When she reached the blow that Long One had struck her in the abdomen, Dobrevski asked her if she knew where the stick which he had struck her was.

'I think he stayed somewhere on the shore or he dropped it in the river.'

'If we go to the place, would you be able to recognise it?'

'Perhaps. I don't know. It happened in the twilight,' Xena said. She didn't want to go back there and told them that.

'Don't you want to help us capture Long One and charge him with attempted murder and murders?'

'Attempted murder?' Xena looked at the two men questioningly.

'From what you're telling us, it goes without saying that he tried to kill you, didn't he?'

'Yes,' she realised. They were looking for her as a witness. Dary and Gal were right. They didn't want to arrest her or accuse her of fraud. They wanted her help.

'I know it's hard for you to talk about it, but we saw the medical records from the A&E. The injuries that Long One inflicted on you were severe, you could have lost your life if your

friend hadn't taken you to the hospital right away and...'
Dobrevski looked at her sadly, 'we know you lost your baby.'

'Yes, that's right,' Xena said softly. She had thrown this hard truth deep into her soul, her recollection causing her pain. Tears streamed down her cheeks again.

'I'm sorry,' said Dobrevski. 'I don't want to upset you but these are the facts. You are a witness, and you can accuse him of attempted murder.'

'I don't want to have anything to do with this man. I don't want to get close to him and his people.'

'Don't you want the truth to come out?' Ivanov asked firmly. 'Your boyfriend is dead, your baby is dead.'

'Do you think I don't know that?' Xena shouted in his face. 'But if they find me, I'll be dead, too.'

'They can't find you,' Dobrevski said.

'Right? And how did they know where I lived then? The moment you found out where I worked and lived, his people were there. In front of my quarters, waiting for me.'

The two men looked at each other.

'What are you talking about?' Ivanov asked her.

'When I last saw Dobrevski, I went to get my things from the apartment. It was full of cops, as were two of Long One's men.'

'Can you describe these people to us?'

'Of course, I know them. I can also tell you their names.'

Dobrevski wrote down the names and Ivanov left the room to check them.

'I'm sorry about that, we didn't know they were there.'

'Isn't it your job to know everything?' Xena asked.

'What we knew was that there was a theft in the apartment where you lived. That's why the police were there. Your roommates found someone digging into their belongings.'

'And you didn't know I lived there?'

'No, we found out after they found your things and one of the girls you lived with declared you were missing,' Dobrevski explained.

'But how did Long One's people know where I lived then? I thought someone from the police told them.'

'We are not from the police. Not exactly. We are an investigative team and we work on several cases simultaneously. We received information about where you work, but we didn't know where you lived.'

'So, they didn't find it from you?' Xena asked.

'No, we are a team of few people, and I trust each of them,' said Dobrevski. 'Long One found you another way, not through us.'

'But how?' Xena asked.

'Probably the same way we found you. Someone recognised you.'

'The world is small,' Xena said softly.

'I have to admit you have a great ability to hide,' Ivanov said, when he returned to the room. 'It usually takes us two or three months to find people like you, but you've been able to hide for a long time and yes, we knew you were using Anna's ID, but by the time we realised it, you had left the country and it was too late to stop you and in another country it's harder to find you. A very good move, I would say that you planned it in advance.'

Xena didn't answer, she wasn't sure if there was a threat in Ivanov's voice. She chose to remain silent. Dobrevski looked at her, smiled slightly and handed her a large envelope.

'Open it,' he told her.

She picked up the envelope but did not open it.

'What's inside?'

'Documents and photos.'

'Why are you giving them to me?' she asked.

'Read them and look at them. It may change your mind to decide to help us.'

'So you won't arrest me?'

'No, you're free to go. I know you have my phone number, but I'll give it to you again just in case. If you decide to help us catch him and put him in prison, call me. Your new ID card and passport are waiting for you at the counter. With your real name, you can use them, from our side no one will cause you problems.'

'And on Long One's side?' Xena asked.

'He certainly already knows that you use Anna's documents, the chance to find you with your name or hers is the same.'

Xena nodded. She began to rise slowly from her chair and then slowly sat down.

'How did it happen?' she asked. 'How did they kill him?'

'Everything is in the documents, there are photos. Take a look at them, read all the reports and you will understand.'

'Anyway, how did this happen?' she asked, looking Dobrevski in the eye.

'He died slowly, if that's what you're asking me. We assume that he was beaten with the same wooden stick that Long One hit you with, the scars from the wounds are almost the same as yours,' he said. His eyes looked at her sadly. He thought that she maybe didn't realise that if it were not for her friend, she would have died slowly and painfully. Her medical record from the hospital and the photos attached to it were horrifying. Xena was lucky to survive.

Xena got up slowly, but this time she left. She headed for the door and turned at the last moment. She looked at the two men looking sad and nodded.

'Thank you,' she said.

They nodded and said nothing. They secretly hoped the information in the envelope would make her call and help them. Otherwise, against her will, they would summon her to court and try to prove the guilt of Long One and one of his men. However, this would take time and they didn't want to delay. They had a better chance with Xena if she got involved in the investigation.

Xena picked up her new documents, left Anna's ID card, walked slowly out of the embassy and looked around. She knew that Dobrevski was right and that Long One's men would soon find her. She didn't have a new identity, she would have to live with her old one and that put her at risk. However, something told her that Dobrevski and Ivanov would be watching her and guarding her for at least the next few days. From what she heard in the room, they needed her, but they didn't specify what exactly they expected her to do. Apparently, they preferred not to issue their cards until she called them and she would call them, she would help them. She had solved it after the fifth minute in the room with these two men. They were right, Long One had tried to kill her, he had killed her baby and the father of her child and she would not leave it at that. If she had the chance, she would destroy him.

Xena returned to her room, and called her boss to say that she would not be able to work tonight. Lisa wasn't happy, but she didn't say it out loud.

Xena made herself tea, picked up a box of biscuits she had bought on her way home, and opened the large brown envelope. Several documents and a pile of photos spilled out of it. The photos were of Ivan's body lying on the river stones on the river bank. His blood had flowed between the stones and dried there. His clothes were dry, Xena thought. When she last saw him, his T-shirt was soaked in blood and water. He must have been dead on the shore for a long time. Her tears flowed from her eyes again. They blurred her gaze, what she saw upset her deeply. Her body began to tremble again, as if she were there, as if she had stepped on the water again, in the cold raging river. Most likely, Long One killed Ivan as soon as Xena escaped. Ivan was right then. She held his life in her hands and allowed him to be killed. Xena's hands relaxed on her lap, the biscuit she had bitten slightly before seeing the pictures had shattered and crumbs could be seen all around her. Xena's tears streamed down the other side of the biscuit and made them soft and wet. However, she didn't pay attention to this. Instead, she looked at the rest of the photos with trembling hands. The place where Ivan was killed was the same place where they had met. Xena saw nothing resembling the stick with which they had fought Long One. She looked at Ivan's body for a while and turned the photos so she couldn't see them. She certainly wouldn't be able to sleep tonight.

Xena decided to take a shower before reading the reports. She wanted to focus and not miss an important detail. If she was going to help the investigative team, she had to be aware of what information they had and consider how she could help them.

After a shower Xena made another peppermint tea, but no dinner. She couldn't eat anything. She felt like vomiting from what she saw. Xena took the photos and put them in the envelope so as not to distract her. Then she picked up a few sheets of paper and began to read.

From what she read, there was nothing to prove or link Long One to the murder. The only thing they had was the testimony of his friend, which a name was not mentioned, according to which Ivan had taken a lot of money from Long One and had not paid his debt. That was the only connection to Long One. Xena was not surprised by the lack of evidence. Long One was smart and also held the Police Station. Everyone obeyed him. Even if there were clues, someone had made sure they were deleted. Xena disappointedly put the reports aside. Dobrevski was right, they needed someone like her. She might accuse him of attempted murder, but she, like them, knew she couldn't prove who had hit her and why. It would be her word against his. On the other hand, if they found that wooden pole he had hit her with, it could change the things.

It was almost midnight when Xena called Dobrevski.

'I'll try to help,' she told him.

'I'm glad to hear it,' his voice was excited, but also somehow tired.

'What's next?' Xena asked.

'Now, we have to prepare you. Pack your bags, please call the nightclub where you work and tell them you will be away for a few months.'

'All right,' Xena said.

'I'll come to pick you up at six in the morning. I know you like to get up early,' he said.

'Obviously you know a lot about me,' she said.

'More than you think,' he said again, a sad note in his voice.

After talking to him, Xena pulled out the pictures of Ivan's body again. She covered his body and stared into his face. He was obviously struggling because his expression was that of a man in pain.

'What did you do, Ivan?' she asked softly. She still didn't understand why he needed all that money. What demons he chased. Here that the Devil had caught up with him and not only with him, but also with their child. Xena looked at the picture a little longer, then put it away. She didn't know what she was getting herself into, but she knew that if she didn't, she and her friends would be in danger forever. She had to get rid of it and try to help get this mobster and his men in prison.

As she had expected, Xena couldn't sleep that night. All she could see were those bloody images. She finally got up and took another shower, hoping she wouldn't wake her roommates. She wrote them a note that she would be absent for several months, but would continue to pay the rent. Then she prepared a bag with the most necessary and important things for her and waited for Dobrevski to call her. Five minutes before six, she saw a car stop in front of her house. At that moment, her phone rang.

'Good morning,' he said. 'Are you ready?'

'Yes, I'm coming now.'

Xena got up, looked around the room one last time and left the house.

In addition to Dobrevski, there were two other men in the car. One was Ivanov, the other was introduced to her as Billy Technique. She never knew if his name was real name or if it was a nickname.

Dobrevski was driving, Ivanov was in the seat next to him and Xena and Billy were in the back seats. Billy handed her hot coffee.

'Drink, you'll need it. We have a long way to go.'

'Are we going to travel by car?' Xena asked.

'No, with a charter flight, but the airport is outside London,' Billy said, smiling slightly at her.

Billy and Dobrevski were around her age. Xena couldn't believe she was being left to young people like them. She expected most of the team to be people of Ivanov's age.

'How did you sleep?' Dobrevski asked her.

'I didn't sleep,' she said.

'Well, you can sleep during the flight.'

'Maybe,' Xena said sluggishly.

Billy pulled out a large laptop and began typing quickly. He didn't even look at the keyboard, he talked to Dobrevski and typed at the same time. Xena looked at him curiously.

'He's taken,' Dobrevski said.

'What?' she asked, puzzled.

'He's married,' he smiled.

'I have no such interest in him,' Xena said, her cheeks burning. She blushed like a high school student. 'I just wondered how he types without even looking at the keyboard.'

'I'm used to it,' Billy said. 'And yes, I'm married. Happily married,' he said and looked at Dobrevski.

'With two children,' Ivanov added and for the first time Xena saw him smiling.

'All right,' Xena said, 'I'll keep that in mind.' The men laughed, apparently deciding what she said was funny.

They travelled for more than an hour. Finally they arrived at a small airport. There a lady waited for them, quickly checked their documents and directed them to one of the small planes. Xena looked at the plane anxiously.

'Don't worry,' Dobrevski told her, seeing her concern.

Xena didn't answer. She followed the men in the small cabin. They made her settle in first and comfortably. She was advised to sleep, so she rested her head on the seat. She felt the plane take off and then fell asleep.

Xena woke up about an hour later. The men talked to each other. They talked about her and where to put her. Apparently, her quick decision surprised them. Dobrevski saw that she had woken up and moved to the seat next to her.

'How are you?' he asked her.

'I am fine. And how are you?'

He smiled.

'I'm fine too. By the way, you can call me Danny.'

'Danny?' Xena stared at him and then she remembered. She knew him. He had been her neighbour many years ago. After a scandal, his parents left town.

'You finally recognised me,' he laughed. There was a gleam in his eyes.

'Yes. You seemed familiar to me, but I couldn't remember where. When you said to call you Danny, I remembered. You were very little when I last saw you.'

She examined him from head to toe. He was a tall man now, no wonder she didn't recognise him. She had last seen him when he was ten years old. She was almost four years older than him.

'Would you have called me earlier if you had remembered who I was?' he asked her.

'Probably not,' she admitted.

'You'd think I was one of Long One's men.'

'Yes. Some of the boys in the neighbourhood became his people. Why shouldn't you be one of them?'

'There's no way,' he said. Something sad passed through his eyes. Xena didn't understand what caused this.

'Did you manage to rest last night?' she asked him.

'I didn't really make it. We had to prepare a lot of things.'

'I see,' Xena said, looking at him again from head to toe. 'You've grown a lot.'

Her words elicited loud laughter on the plane. Xena laughed too, realising how ridiculous her words were. Danny moved back to the men,who kept telling him how much he had grown.

Xena leaned back in her seat. Danny had been one of her childhood friends. She couldn't believe she didn't recognise him right away. He and his brother were among the few children who played with her. Until they left the town surprisingly. Their grandparents died shortly afterwards. Xena was calm, she believed Danny, there was no way this boy she knew at the time had turned into a bad person. She looked at him again. Dary was right, he had become handsome. The girls must have chased him.

The landing of the plane interrupted her thoughts. Danny moved close to her again.

'We'll be landing soon. We will go to a training base in the mountains.'

'What are we going to do there?' Xena asked.

'We will train. I have to be sure that if something unforeseen happens you will be able to defend yourself.'

'I have been training in karate for some time.'

Danny looked at her and said, 'You don't stop surprising me, Xena!'

'I can still take a few more lessons,' she laughed.

'In addition to karate, I will have to teach you to observe people and also to make a plan.'

'What plan?'

'We need a confession to murder or attempted murder.'

'Okay and you want me to make him admit it?'

'Yes, we'll be close to you, but you have to challenge him to admit it. Long One is more dangerous than you imagine, so we will have to prepare you well and give our team time to prepare everything to protect you.'

Xena was silent for a while.

'Have you been back there?'

'To our hometown? Yes, several times. Last time for work. If it makes you feel better, no one recognises me.' Danny gave her a slight smile.

'Yes, I'm ashamed I didn't immediately remember who you were.'

'I'm grown up,' he said with a lovely smile.

'Yes. You grew up.'

The plane landed and everyone prepared to disembark. Ivanov approached Xena and said, 'You'll stay with Danny at this base for a while. We will prepare everything and we can join you when Danny says you are ready.'

'All right. See you soon,' Xena said.

Xena and Danny drove to the base in an old car. Along the way, they talked about the past, remembering people and events. They were in a very good mood.

'Why did you move?' Xena asked.

'We had no choice,' Danny said. 'But I'll tell you about it another time. It's not something I want to talk about right now.'

'And your brother? Is he okay?'

'He's fine. He's a math teacher at a school, married without children.'

'Good for him. Why are you in this agency?'

'I've wanted to catch the bad guys since I was little,' he smiled.

'Apparently you are good, out of the respect I see in your colleagues.'

'Yes, I have quite successful actions.'

'Is that what you call them, actions? Am I an action too?' Xena asked.

'No, your case is different. It's as important to you as it is to me.'

As they walked, Xena caught sight of a large modern building that clashed with the beautiful nature surrounding them. They were deep in the mountains. Pines rose from all sides and covered part of the building. This obviously provided good cover for the training base. Xena picked up her jacket and followed Danny. No one met them. Danny used a plastic card and a code to enter the building. It was quiet inside, as if no one was there, but from the cars parked in front, Xena guessed that there were at least a dozen people there.

Danny led her to her room and told her to rest for a while. Xena decided to take advantage and although she had taken two showers in less than ten hours, she decided to take one more now. It was as if she could clean all that filth from her body and hair. She put on sports clothes, as she decided that they would most likely start training immediately. She was almost ready when Danny knocked on her door. He used the signal they had as children and it made her smile. She opened the door for him and to her surprise saw that he was wearing a shirt and a suit.

'I thought we were going to train,' she said.

'Not now. Now I'm going to take you to a nearby town for lunch and buy you some things.'

Xena smiled, invited him into the room and he waited for her to change. A little later, they sat facing each other in a small restaurant and talked.

'Do you take all the women you train here?' she asked him.

'Actually, no,' he smiled. 'You're the first. We usually eat at the base with the others. We've known each other for a long time, that's why we're here.'

'It's nice.'

'Yes, I like coming here. The food is very good.'

'That's right,' Xena agreed.

'Are you worried?' he asked her.

'Yes, I don't know what to expect and that worries me.'

'I can tell you what awaits you in the next two weeks. You will train, talk to a psychologist and make a plan for the future.'

Xena nodded. At least she knew what would happen next.

'Can I ask you something?'

'Ask,' he said.

'I really want to see Gal and Dary. Is there any chance I can see them?'

'I don't think it's a good idea.'

'Still, I'd feel better if I saw them, at least for a while.'

'Alright. I'll see what I can do, but I can't promise. Your meeting could put us all at risk.'

Xena paused. She didn't want anyone to get hurt, but she missed her friends and if she had at least a small chance of seeing them, she would take advantage of it.

'And one more thing,' she said. 'Do you have any idea why Ivan borrowed money from Long One?'

'Don't you know?' Danny asked her. His gaze darkened.

'I did ask him then, you know in the river, but he didn't say anything,' Xena said, stopping to eat. She watched him expectantly. He hesitated to answer her, but her gaze was insistent and finally he said, 'The money was for a woman.'

'Which woman?' Xena asked.

'You won't like the answer,' he warned her.

'Which woman did he take the money for?' Xena raised her voice unconsciously. The people at the other tables turned, drawn by her words.

Danny leaned close to her and said, 'Adi.'

'Adi?' Xena's eyes widened. Surprise gripped her body. 'Are you sure?'

'I told you that you wouldn't like the answer.'

'But why did Adi need money and why didn't they both tell me?'

Xena understood the answer only from Danny's gaze.

'Were they lovers? Behind my back?'

Danny nodded.

'But...' Xena began but didn't continue. She thought fast. So Adi accused her of murder and didn't protect her.

'What was the money for?' Xena asked.

Danny was silent. He didn't want to tell her. He knew she would guess. The truth blinded her. Adi loved glamorous things. She often dated different men who bought her expensive gifts. Ivan borrowed money to court her and had pledged not to her but to Xena if he failed to return the money.

'Are you okay?' Danny asked her.

'Honestly no, I'm not well. I want to go to my room.'

He didn't object. They had to buy essentials for Xena but decided it was better to postpone it until the next day. Danny paid the bill and tried to help Xena get up from her chair. She roughly rejected his hand, stood alone and walked to the door without looking at him. She hated all the men and women in the world right now. She didn't want to, but her tears came again.

That's how everyone will remember me; tearful, crying every five minutes, she thought bitterly. They didn't talk in the car, her thoughts still jumping from one incident to another. Everything was in front of her and she just didn't want to see it before.

'Can I do something to make you feel better?' Danny asked her in front of her room.

'No. Sorry for my behavior in the restaurant. I was in shock.'

'I know. No problem. If you need to talk to someone, call me. My room is at the end of the hallway.'

'Thanks. I'd prefer to be alone and make sense of things.'

'I'll see you tomorrow morning. I'll come pick you up at six-thirty and show you around the base.'

'Thank you, Danny. Good night!'

'Good night!' he said, waiting for her to enter her room. He felt very sorry for Xena. He didn't like telling her about Ivan and Adi, but it was better to tell her now than if she found out later. Although, he always thought she knew. The shock had shaken her. Danny decided not to go back to his room yet, he just changed and went to the gym. Sport allowed him to ease the tension. He wondered how Xena could handle what she had just learned.

Xena was in the shower again. The running water flowed with her tears. She was squatting, the warm water flooding her and dulling the sound of her hiccups. She was so shocked by the discovery that her boyfriend and her best friend had been seeing each other behind her back that she didn't know how to cope with the pain. Her closest people had betrayed her. Adi's greed had driven Ivan mad and they had thrown Xena to the wolves. Somehow, her soul couldn't stand it. This called into question all her friendships. Whether Dary and Gal were also her friends? Was it worth risking her life and their lives just to see them and talk to them briefly? No, it wasn't worth it. Moreover, Dary was pregnant and it might put her at risk. Was there any such thing as friendship at all? All these questions and thoughts quickly raced through her mind. Xena began to wonder if it wasn't really her problem? But she knew she wasn't in it. It was in her past and she had to forget it, clear it and erase it.

A loud noise startled her. Someone was pounding on the door. She forced herself to get up and see what was happening. At first, she didn't know who was knocking, then she recognised Danny's voice. She wrapped herself in a large towel and opened the door slightly.

'Are you okay?' he asked her.

'Yes, I took a shower.'

'You've been taking a shower for two hours,' Danny said reproachfully. 'I got worried about you.' He really did look worried.

'I'm so sorry. I didn't know that so much time had passed.'

'Do you feel better?'

'Yes, I feel better now. I will get dressed and go to bed. Sorry for bothering you.'

'If you feel bad, call me,' he said anxiously.

'I'll definitely call you. I'm fine, don't worry.'

'All right.'

'All right. Good night!'

'Good night!' Danny said, though he was convinced it wouldn't be easy for either of them. She would grieve the infidelity of her friends and he would worry about her.

162

Xena fell asleep only after midnight. She slept soundly until six-thirty when Danny knocked on her door.

'Good morning,' he said.

'Good morning,' she said. 'I'm sorry, I just woke up. Give me ten minutes to prepare.'

'No problem,' Danny said and returned to his room. Xena sounded reassured, he thought. Ten minutes later she was waiting for him in the hallway. She looked tired, but somehow calmer. Apparently her crying had worked well.

Danny took her first to the dining room, where they drank coffee, tea and had breakfast. They were both very hungry. They were joined by two people - a man and a woman. They would be in charge of some of Xena's training exercises. The woman was tall, blonde, with blue eyes and a sporty figure. Her name was Karina. Her interest was in Danny, who, however, did not respond to her glances. Xena thought there might be something between them. The man named Emil was older than them, probably in his late forties, also in good shape. Xena was told about the different stages of training she had to go through.

After breakfast, Danny led her to show her the base. Most of the rooms were equipped with training equipment. Others were used for massage or relaxation. Xena liked the base very much. It was big and made like for the training of Olympians. Their tour ended with a small stadium at the back of the building, as well as a Zen garden, which Xena liked.

'It's calming, isn't it?' Xena told Danny.

'Yes, I come here often.'

'Danny, can I ask you something personal?'

'Of course,' he said, turning in anticipation.

'Do you have friends?'

'Of course I have. You have already met one of them. Billy is one of my best friends.'

'And out of work?'

Danny was silent for a moment.

'I don't have many friends outside of work. Why do you ask?'

'Out of curiosity.'

'Does it have anything to do with Ivan and Adi?' he asked her.

'Yes and no. I just thought that with this job you can hardly make friends.'

'That's right, it's hard, but I have one or two friends from my teenage years. We rarely see each other, but I'm glad to see them when I can.'

Xena sat down on one of the benches in the Zen garden. Danny sat down next to her.

'You are not to blame yourself for what happened to Ivan, you know that?' he told her.

'I know and I still don't understand. My best friend and my boyfriend. Sorry, I'm getting you into my dramas again.'

'I understand what you're going through and I can't give you answers. I myself was shocked when I learned and I hardly knew them.'

'Yes, I find it hard to believe, but last night after I took a shower I remembered the last few months before Long One killed

Ivan. In fact, the signs that something was wrong were there, but I didn't want to see them.'

Danny didn't know what to say, he preferred to let her talk. He knew from experience that grief didn't melt so quickly. It would take Xena months to rethink what had happened and unfortunately she would have to hear more unpleasant things, but Danny decided that now was neither the time nor the place to share them with her. She needed time, he too. A few minutes in the Zen garden made Xena calmer. They turned the conversation to the two-week programme and the schedule she had to follow. In general, the people here had planned every minute of her stay at the base and her training began at noon.

The first week seemed exhausting to Xena. From morning to night she went from one workout to another, with breaks for breakfast, lunch and dinner, as well as massages and aromatherapy. Danny attended and partnered with her in some of the training sessions, in others she was alone or with another student at her level. Xena thought that with the karate training she had taken before, she was healthy and strong, but now she realised that it was not enough. Danny taught her easy grip strikes for knocking down the enemy and the psychological struggle with the unmoving gaze. He seemed to be doing his best to help her with her studies.

'We won't leave here until you pass the exams,' he told her.

'How long did it take the others to pass this stage?' she asked him.

'It's different, depending on gender and age. Some took ten days, others took more than a month.'

Xena trained and studied hard. She sincerely hoped these skills would not be useful to her. It all depended on how Long One would react when he saw her. The plan was for her to return to Vedna and challenge him, but she might not succeed. According to Danny, Long One already knew he was under investigation for the murder and he would probably be very cautious. Especially if he decided to talk to Xena. She had to challenge him in some way and that in itself meant trouble.

Xena decided to concentrate on training and not think about what they would do next. Thoughts of Ivan, Adi and Long One distracted her and Xena did her best not to think about them, at least for the moment. She liked to play sports, there was no problem in that respect, but the conversations she had to have with people about her life made her nervous. She didn't like talking about herself to strangers and she didn't see how talking to someone while lying on the sofa would help her. She could say everything to Rurko. At least he understood her, at least she thought so and most importantly, he didn't ask questions. Xena was nervous about all the psycho-tests that they made her fill out. This part of the training was not fun at all. The dojo felt more comfortable. Unfortunately, everyone told her that until she passed all the stages of training and passed all the tests, she would not be allowed to leave the training base. So Xena did her best to do whatever was required of her.

She saw Danny less and less. He often travelled outside the base and of course, did not tell her what was happening. She felt calm when he was around, but when he didn't come back all day, she began to feel anxious. Xena didn't know him well, but she trusted him. Her intuition told her that he would do anything to protect her. When he didn't return in the evening, Xena couldn't sleep all night.

She got up early one morning and knocked on his door. No one answered, no one was in the room. She decided to take a walk and went to the Zen garden. There she always felt calm and in harmony. When it was time for breakfast, she headed straight for the dining room. Someone called her name and she turned. She stopped in surprise. Danny, Gal and Dary walked across from her. She rushed to them and hugged Dary tightly first, whose pregnancy was already visible.

'I can't believe you brought them here,' she told Danny with a wide smile.

'I told you I'd try my best for you to see them,' he smiled broadly.

Gal picked her up and turned her around. He was strong and mature. He had become a man during the time since they had seen each other.

'I missed you so much,' he told her, kissing her forehead and cheeks. He wouldn't let her go until he had to back away. Xena led them back to the garden. She was hungry and needed some coffee, but she would wait.

'I'll change and take a shower,' Danny told them.

Dary and Gal followed him with their eyes.

'I told you to talk to him,' Dary said at last and then added, 'Handsome'.

'I told you too.' Gal laughed.

'Yes, you were both right as always. Tell me now what is happening to you, to the nightclub, to the baby. Do you already know the gender?'

'Yes, it will be a boy,' Dary said happily.

As Danny looked on, the three of them talked. They had a lot to say to each other. An hour passed imperceptibly. Danny brought coffee and then returned with food. He felt like he was hosting a meeting with good friends. Xena and her friends kept telling each other stories. All three looked very happy. Danny wished he had such friends too, but his job kept him from getting close to people. It was dangerous for him and for them. Sometimes he regretted doing just that. Of course, he could have given up and looked for work elsewhere, but at least for now he didn't feel the need. Or at least he didn't feel it until he met Xena. He looked at her, she beamed. She was telling a story and laughing almost hysterically. The woman who was crying in the shower was gone, replaced by a cheerful young woman whose friends clearly adored her. Danny was sure Gal was in love with her. His gaze was distracted and clearly showed his feelings. Xena, however, seemed to have no idea about it. She gave him a friendly hug, nothing in her demeanor suggested that she had the same feelings for the young man. Danny was almost jealous, she was much more reserved with him. She trusted him, but she didn't share anything. She was focused on her studies and rarely had long conversations with him and Danny wanted to change that.

The three friends talked for another hour. In the end, Danny had to interrupt them. It was time to take the guests back to their homes. Xena was visibly sad. He realised that she wished she could see Gal and Dary every day, talk to them on the phone, to send them pictures, but she knew that, at least for now that was impossible.

After a long farewell, her friends left and Xena was left alone again in the Zen garden. She called Danny. He came over with a questioning look.

'Are you coming back tonight?' she asked him.

'Yes, I'll just drop them back and come back. Why? Is something bothering you?'

'No. I just feel calmer when I know you're around,' she admitted.

'I'll call you when I get back,' he told her, touching her cheek lightly. 'Don't worry, you're safe here.'

'I know,' she nodded.

Danny left and she stared after him. She was sure he had done his best to bring Gal and Dary here and she was very grateful to him for that. However, his touch puzzled her. She didn't expect such tenderness from him. Rather, she expected only the concern that an old friend felt toward a friend in need.

Xena went back to reality and to the next workout, then had a massage. The day passed unexpectedly. Danny walked past her to tell her he was back and would be in his room to rest. Apparently, he hadn't slept for a day because he looked very tired.

Xena finished the exercises she had to do for the day and went back to her room. She took a shower and relaxed in bed. She had taken a picture of herself, Dary and Gal with her phone. She was wrong about her friends. Not everyone was a traitor and not everyone would do what Ivan and Adi did. She was glad that there were people who would risk their lives just to come and see her.

There was a knock on her door and she recognised Danny's signal.

'Did you rest well?' she asked him.

'Yes,' though he didn't, he still couldn't sleep.

'Are you hungry?' he asked her.

'Yes,' she laughed.

'If I take you to that restaurant again, will you promise not to make a scene this time?'

'I promise.'

Xena changed quickly. They entered the restaurant and ordered their daily special.

'Do you drink alcohol?' Danny asked.

'No, I don't drink. All I do is watch people pour themselves into it and get drunk all night. What about you?'

'No. I prefer to have control over myself. It's not just about work. I just don't like the feeling of weightlessness.'

'So you got drunk?' Xena asked.

'Several times,' Danny said with a smile. 'I was not a pleasant sight and I fought a lot. Every time I came back home with wounds.'

'So drinking is not good for you?'

'You could say that,' he laughed. 'I'm definitely not the same person when I'm drunk.'

'Will you tell me why you brought me to this restaurant?' she asked him.

'I decided that we both need a little variety and to go beyond the sterile environment at the base.'

'Aren't you afraid someone will recognise us?'

'No, only proven people work in the restaurant.'

'Well, it's at your service.'

'Something like that,' he said. 'But they cook better, don't they?'

'That's right,' she agreed.

'The coaches said you were doing very well. However, the counsellor is not satisfied.'

'I can't talk to him.'

'You have visited a psychologist before. Gal told me,' he answered her questioning look.

'Well, he wasn't exactly a psychologist, he was someone who listened to me.'

'Can't ours listen to you?' he asked her.

"No, my therapist's ears were fluffy.' Xena laughed and told him about Rurko.

'Well, Gal forgot to tell me that detail,' he said.

'Because it's a secret. You can't tell anyone.'

'Alright,' he promised. 'But that doesn't change the fact that you can't do it and they won't let you go until you make some progress.'

She paused. They continued to eat in silence for a few minutes and finally, she said, 'I haven't been able to share my life with strangers since I was a child. I only shared it with Ivan and Adi. Now to some extent with Gal and Dary. Also, with you, if you haven't noticed, but with a complete stranger sitting behind a desk and asking personal questions. I don't think it will work, Danny. That's just not my approach.'

'How about taking a few tests to see how stable you are?' he asked her.

'Do you consider me unstable?' she wondered.

'Not me, but the counsellor. You're not going to kick me out of the restaurant again, are you?'

Xena looked around, she had raised her voice and the people at the next table looked at them.

'I'm sorry, I had no intention of attracting attention.'

'That's what I am talking about. You are not unstable, but you are careless. You get nervous quickly. We have to put out the fire. Do you want to pass these tests?'

'Of course,' she said.

'Then try to calm down. Before we leave the base, I need to make sure you're stable and that I can count on you. I don't want you to be in a dangerous or awkward situation just because you lost your temper.'

Danny's voice was insistent. He had never spoken to her like that before. Of course, Xena knew he was right. She had to focus and stop just feeling sorry for herself, it could get her in trouble.

On their way back from the restaurant, Danny told her that he would not take her to that restaurant again.

'Why? The food was very tasty,' she said with regret.

'Because thanks to you, everyone there already knows us,' he told her. 'But the good news is that there are two more restaurants in the area and next time we will visit one of them.'

Xena turned and smiled.

'I don't want to get you in trouble,' she said.

'You're not causing me trouble. We need to work harder on your concentration. If in the next few days I raise my voice, don't take it personally, it will be part of your training. I have to teach you to control yourself and even if someone shouts at you, you have to stay calm. And talk to the counsellor, please. I have nowhere to find a dog counsellor.'

'Okay, I'll try.'

When they arrived at the base, everyone was alone in their rooms. Xena tried not to give into her feelings. Danny confused her. He was sometimes gentle, sometimes too strict. Although she was sure of one thing, he was right, she was exploding too fast and she couldn't control herself. She had to work on it. Xena slept peacefully that night, knowing he was in the building.

The next few days were busy. Xena managed to pass all the physical tests, but the mental ones didn't allow her to. According to the doctor, she was not ready.

'I told you it would be a problem,' Danny reminded her.

'Yes, you told me.'

They were sitting in the Zen garden, watching the raindrops running down the flower stalks. The murmur of the small fountain soothed her and she liked to stand near it.

'How do you manage to pass these tests?' she asked.

'I went through longer training. Sometimes training can reduce some of the stress, but I often read a book or listen to music to calm down.'

'Is it that simple?' she asked.

'No, but maybe you should try it. What calmed you down when your grandmother died?'

'Running, I went to the stadium and ran for hours.'

'I remember you with red sports gear.'

Xena laughed. He unconsciously took her back in time.

'Maybe you should try again and run,' he suggested. 'The stadium is free early in the morning. If you want I'll come and run with you.'

'No, I have to be alone. It won't stop me from trying, will it?' she said.

'No, it won't.'

Xena took Danny's advice and started running early in the morning at the small stadium. Sometimes it seemed to her that she was back in her hometown and that someone was watching her. The fresh air calmed her. Also the atmosphere around. It was quiet everywhere. She heard her footsteps and counted *one, two, three, four*. Sometimes Danny would come at the last minute and join her for the final sprint. It became their habit.

'You're talking to yourself while you're running,' he said one morning.

'Yes, I count to four.'

'Interesting tactic. Who told you about it?'

'I don't know. It's like I've been doing it since I was a child. It's become a habit, I don't even realise sometimes that I do it.'

'I hum,' he admitted.

'What do you hum?' she asked.

'If I tell you, you'll make fun of me,' he laughed sincerely.

'I won't make fun of you,' she promised.

He looked at her seriously, wondering whether to tell her or not.

'Do you remember the children's song about the cat and the mouse, which they sometimes made us sing at school?'

'Yes. Do you hum that song?'

'Yes.'

Xena burst out laughing sincerely.

'Really?' she asked.

'You promised not to make fun of me,' he reminded her.

'I'm not making fun of you. I'm laughing at you,' she said and she kept giggling as she returned to her room.

'I knew I couldn't count on your word,' he said after her.

'You can, this is our secret from now on,' Xena continued to laugh at him. Something made her challenge him. She didn't usually treat people like that, but he was different.

A few days later, Xena felt calm and confident enough to take the test, although she couldn't pass it. They didn't explain why, they just told her she wasn't ready yet. That made her nervous. She went back to her room and didn't leave until late in the afternoon. She took a shower and went to the Zen garden. She was ready to give up, there was nothing more she could do to make these people happy. Danny joined her in silence. They didn't talk, they just sat and watched the water flowing from the fountain.

'The run didn't work,' he told her.

'I know,' she said softly.

'Can I offer you something?'

'Of course.'

'Stop thinking about it and stop overloading. You need something to calm you down.'

'Maybe meditation.'

'Perhaps. You said you practiced karate for a while. How does kata work for you?'

'Very well. It calmed me down,' she said.

'Great, come with me then. I'll show you one or two katas that I use sometimes.'

He headed for one of the gyms and she followed. She was wearing jeans, but decided not to change. The clothes didn't matter in this case.

Danny stood in the middle of the room and gestured for her to stand beside him. He took a step forward, she followed his movements. The kata he showed her was long. When it was over, they bowed and started a new one. Then they repeated the first one. It took them several hours to do everything in sync. At the end of the day, Danny suggested they continue with a ten-minute committee.

Xena was unexpectedly fast. She managed to hit him a few times, which surprised Danny. She had really trained a lot. She was flexible and could easily turn in any direction. A worthy opponent, Danny thought. Near the end of the training, Xena fell in an attempt to avoid one of his blows. Her knee ached and she gasped in pain. Danny rushed to the rescue, took her leg, and tried to see if it was broken by feeling each bone. Reassured that it was nothing serious, he leaned over her and whispered in her ear, 'Watch where you step.'

He looked at her, slightly mockingly, 'You didn't think you'd beat me, did you?'

'It hurts, and you triumph,' Xena told him, but when she saw his gaze she laughed. 'If I hadn't fallen, I would have defeated you.'

'Yes, you hope so.' Danny helped her to her feet. She did not dare to stand on her foot.

'Does it hurt?'

'A little.'

'We'll put ice on it and it will be fine by tomorrow. I think we overdid it today,' he said examining her from head to toe. It was as if he appreciated her. 'You're tough,' he finally said.

She nodded. She began to feel uncomfortable with his gaze. His closeness worried her. His muscular body and his gaze made her feel like a little girl.

'I'm going,' she said, 'to look for some ice for my foot.'

'Okay, I'll be waiting for you in the dining room for dinner in half an hour.'

Xena nodded and limped towards the kitchen, where she guessed they could serve her ice. She needed a lot of ice, not just for her knee, but for her whole body.

Half an hour later, Xena stepped more calmly to her feet and entered the dining room. She looked for Danny and saw him talking to Ivanov.

'Hello,' the newcomer greeted her.

'Hello. I thought you wouldn't be joining us yet.'

'It's time. At least according to Danny,' Ivanov said.

'Danny thinks I'm not ready yet.'

'On the contrary,' Danny joined the conversation. 'After today's training I think you are completely ready.'

'And the tests?' she asked.

'What tests?' he grinned.

'You made them up.'

'Not exactly. You passed them the first time, but I decided you needed a little more time.'

'It's hard for Danny to be apart from you,' Ivanov teased.

'Nothing of the kind. I wanted to make sure she could do it.'

'Good,' Xena interrupted. 'Now what? What is expected of me?'

'Now you will get a day off and then we will go to Vedna.'

'Great. Where am I supposed to rest? Here?' she asked.

'No, I have a better idea. We're going to see your bartender. It's time to get out of the dark and expose yourself to a little light.'

'When are we leaving?' Xena asked enthusiastically.

'Tomorrow morning. It will take us three and a half hours to get there,' said Danny.

'Will you come with me?' Xena wondered.

'I told you, he's afraid to let you go,' Ivanov said.

Danny didn't even look at him.

'I want to know you're safe and even though your friend has good security at the nightclub, I would prefer to come with you. Will this be a problem?'

'No,' Xena said and headed for the counter to get something to eat.

'She's beautiful,' Ivanov said.

'That's right,' Danny agreed.

They fell silent and waited for Xena to come with her dinner. Then they all ate in silence, each absorbed in their thoughts.

Xena couldn't sleep with excitement most of the night. It was one thing to stand in the shadows with Long One's people looking for her, it was another to just show up at her former job with her real name, without makeup, without hiding, as if nothing had happened. Long One wasn't stupid, he would surely suspect that something was wrong. However, Xena decided to trust Danny's intuition. She got up in the morning and they made the final sprint together, had breakfast, drank coffee and left for Sofia shortly after ten o'clock.

Along the way, they talked about the past, the river and how they both loved fishing there. They both missed Vedna.

Danny and Xena arrived in Sofia in the early afternoon and settled in a house near Gal's nightclub. Xena was impatient and immediately went to the nightclub. Danny followed her half an hour later. There was already a man from his office taking care of her safety.

Gal was happy to see her. He hugged her again and turned around. He was surprised that she had come to the nightclub and when he didn't see Danny accompanying her, he decided that Xena had refused to help him.

'Danny will be here later. I just couldn't wait to come see you, walk around and stand at the bar.'

'The bar is yours as long as you want it,' Gal told her.

'I have some things to do before I come back. In fact, I'm only here for a few hours and I'm only allowed to stay in your nightclub. I can't leave without Danny.'

'Sure,' Gal said disappointed. 'I was already making plans to take you to dinner.'

'It won't be tonight, but when it's all over, I won't refuse a nice dinner.'

'How are you?' he asked her. She was standing behind the bar. He was sitting opposite her on one of the bar stools.

'I'm fine. Tense. I'm scared, to be honest.'

'Then don't do it.'

'I have to do it, Gal. I don't want to hide forever.'

'I understand. I'm afraid for you too. Does Danny think you can do it?'

'You can ask him in person when he comes.'

Gal heard a new tone in her voice as she spoke of Danny. She didn't speak of him as a stranger, but as a relative.

'Did you get close,' he said, then added, 'with Danny?'

'In fact, we have know each other from our childhood. I last saw him when he was ten, so I didn't recognise him right away. He has changed.'

'Obviously he built muscles,' Xena heard Gal's sarcasm.

'Don't be mean. Danny is a good man,' she said.

'That's right. I'm not saying he's a bad person, but he's muscular,' said Gal, giving her a smile.

Danny's entry into the club interrupted their conversation. The two men greeted each other like old friends and sat together at the bar. Xena continued to stand behind the bar and talk to them for a while. Then she apologised and went to the toilet.

Gal made sure Xena couldn't see or hear them then he turned to Danny and slapped him slightly on the shoulder.

'I see how you look at her. If you hurt her...' Gal didn't finish.

'I'm not going to hurt her,' Danny said, rubbing his shoulder. 'But you know that wherever we go, they don't wish her well.'

'Don't shift the topic. You know very well what I mean,' Gal said.

Danny looked at him, but didn't answer. What the bartender said was a surprise, but now that he thought about it, Gal was right. Danny had begun more than a friendship with Xena, which was now rather dangerous. He had to master it, he thought and he remembered what his grandfather had said, "sometimes we need an outlook, to tell us how we really feel." The old man said it on another occasion, but Danny now understood the truth in his words. He was becoming more attached to Xena than to anyone else he'd known in the last ten years. The fact that she was four years older didn't stop him from thinking of her as a woman. Ivanov was right, she was beautiful and flexible, Danny recalled.

He went behind the bar, made a coffee and then sat down next to Gal again.

'You're right,' he told him.

'Of course I'm right. Do you know how she looks at you? It's like you're Apollo.'

'Really?' Danny wondered.

'Don't pretend you don't know it. You know very well what I'm talking about.'

Xena returned to the bar and the two men began talking about football. She listened to them argue about which team was better.

What she would give for it to be her daily routine. Drink coffee with friends and listen to them talk.

When it was time for the nightclub to open, Xena and Danny said goodbye to Gal. He wished them luck and made them promise to send him a message when it was all over.

Gal's heart sank. Although he was angry with Danny and thought he was his competition, he was worried about both of them. He liked them and felt close to them.

Xena and Danny stepped out the back door of the nightclub and headed for the house they had rented. When they arrived they saw that someone had stocked the fridge with food and drink. They sat down and dined in silence. Neither of them wanted to raise the issue of what was to come tomorrow.

'Gal is very worried, isn't he?' Xena asked.

'More than he shows,' Danny agreed. 'And you, Xena, are you worried?'

He looked her straight in the eye and that bothered her. She could barely swallow her food.

'Just thinking that I have to talk to Long One makes me angry,' she admitted.

'Promise me you'll tell me if you panic.' Danny looked at her intently.

'All right,' she said, at last.

'It's important, Xena!'

'I know, you're right. If I'm scared, I'll tell you right away. When are we leaving?'

'At midnight,' he said, 'it's better if fewer people see us arrive in case anyone recognises me. We will stay at the hotel next to the stadium. My team and I will be in the next two rooms of yours, so there will be less chance for someone to jump over and come to you. Only you will go out. I, Billy and Ivanov will stay at the hotel.'

'But then…' Xena began, but fell silent.

'Who will guard you? Is that what you wanted to ask me?'

'Yes.'

'We have people in the town who will follow you and who will watch you. For everyone's safety it is better not to know who they are.'

Xena nodded and began to eat again and so did Danny. There was some tension between them, but they both pretended it didn't exist. Instead, they turned their thoughts to the next few days.

'I'll take a shower and go to bed for a few hours,' Xena said.

'All right. I'll wake you when it's time to go.'

Danny was worried, he looked out the window from time to time to see if anyone was watching the house and the car. He knew that their colleagues were guarding them and yet he felt obligated to check. Outside, everything seemed calm. People had gathered in front of the nightclub, as always, there was a queue of people wanting to go in for a drink. Gal knew how to attract customers. Danny stepped away from the window and opened his laptop. He still had a lot to clarify with Billy and Ivanov. He started chatting with them. He didn't want to talk to Xena and it was better for her to sleep before they left. Insomnia was a daily occurrence for him but it would hurt her.

Xena had felt calm and safe, and fell asleep in the first minute after Danny had left her.

Danny woke her just before midnight.

'We have to leave in ten minutes,' he told her.

'Alright. I'll just change.'

She looked sleepy, with tousled hair and slightly reddened eyes.

'You'll be able to sleep again after we check into the hotel.'

Xena nodded. She had been deeply asleep and waking up this time was slow. Danny made her a strong coffee, took their bags, and put them into the car. A few minutes after midnight they left for their hometown, each of them immersed in memories and thoughts. The village brought bad memories for both of them. Xena wondered what it was like for him to go back there. She knew there was something deeper in his story, but he had never explained it.

Surprisingly, there was traffic on the motorway even at that hour. When they turned off the motorway it was completely dark. It was as if they were the only two people in the world. The intimate atmosphere in the car intensified this feeling. Xena thought that under other circumstances she would be happy to travel with him on a long journey. They obviously liked each other and why not, she thought, there was no other person on Earth who understood how she felt.

When they arrived in Vedna the town was asleep. No one could be seen around the hotel. Danny parked quickly, picked up the luggage and entered the building. Xena followed. There was no one in the lobby and she guessed that someone had arranged that so no one could see them when they entered. Her room was on the third floor overlooking the mountain. She left her suitcase, opened the balcony, took a deep breath of the familiar fresh air and then returned. She couldn't sleep, so she sat down in one of the armchairs and waited there until dawn.

Ten minutes before six, she put on her sports gear and as Danny and she had agreed, she left the hotel and ran to the empty stadium. She experienced *deja vu*, running alone again, hearing her footsteps and counting *one, two, three, four*. After a while the birds woke up and began to sing their beautiful songs. The town was also waking up. The cafe gradually filled with people and Xena saw little dumb onlookers watching her run. They didn't even hide their curiosity. Nothing had changed in their habits, she recalled. They would observe and comment on why and how she had returned to the town. She did a few more laps, sprinted the last one and headed for the hotel. On the way she waved to her fellow citizens and they waved her back. Just like that spring day a few years ago, Xena thought.

According to the plan, when the people saw her running, someone would notify Long One of her return to the village and he would most likely look for her at the hotel.

'Why do I have to be in a hotel?' Xena asked when she realised she had to stay there. 'My house is empty, so is your grandparents' place.'

The mention of his grandparents darkened Danny's eyes. Or so it seemed to her.

'We can keep you safe at the hotel. It's more dangerous in your house. There are many other houses nearby and many people coming in and out walking down the street. The hotel is isolated and if we are in the adjoining rooms there is less chance of someone ambushing you.'

Xena nodded understandingly. She really wanted to go home and get some of her favorite things but she realised the danger had suppressed her desire. After jogging, she entered the hotel, ordered breakfast and coffee and then asked for it to be taken to her room. The girl at the front desk was unknown to her. She looked about eighteen and maybe that's why Xena didn't know her. She was young. Xena waited for her order to be recorded and walked up to the third floor, though Danny had advised her to take the elevator. Xena didn't believe that Long One would look for her today or that he would send people to her immediately. He was cautious, he would investigate the situation first and then act.

Xena went back to her room, took a quick shower and then drank a coffee that had been left for her by Danny or one of his colleagues. Then she stared at the mountain. She didn't know what to expect but she wouldn't stay here locked up and wait for hours. She would go out and walk around the town; she could even eat somewhere.

After breakfast was brought to her by the hotel staff, Xena knocked on the wall and motioned for Danny to join her. She knew they had cameras everywhere in the hotel and she guessed that Danny had already seen that the floor was empty. A minute later he joined her and they had breakfast together talking about some of the people they had seen in the cafe.

Danny was well acquainted with the local gossip, Xena thought. Apparently, he hasn't been that far in recent years. She might even have seen him around town, but with his new look, she would hardly have recognised him.

'I want to walk around the town,' she told him.

'Where do you want to go?' he asked her. There was no resistance or wonder in his voice. Apparently he had expected her to leave the hotel.

'I don't know, I haven't decided yet.'

'Before you go out, you have to tell us the route and stick to it.'

Their eyes met. They didn't talk about it, but there was definitely tension between them. Danny looked at her worriedly.

'You know it's dangerous. I need to make sure you're safe,' he explained.

'Okay, I'll think about it and tell you where I'm going.'

Danny sighed visibly relieved. For him, this was the most difficult task so far in his career. To be in his hometown with a woman who was obviously attracted to him and to be threatened by the most hated man he knew. Billy was right, it wasn't going to work out well one way or another. Ivanov and Billy, as his closest friends, had immediately sensed his fascination with Xena. Gal had sensed it, Danny thought, so engrossed that he couldn't control himself. He tried to divert his thoughts, and gave Xena a sheet of paper and a pen, and asked her to make a route. When she was ready, he took the sheet, looked at it with his worried look and said to her, 'Remember, don't deviate under any circumstances. Whatever happens, you stick to what you wrote.'

'I promise,' she said.

Danny's anxiety had infected Xena. He was right, she didn't have to move just like that, it was dangerous even in front of the hotel. However, she knew Long One somewhat and she knew that until he saw her with his own eyes he would not look for her. Standing and waiting in the hotel would only make her nervous and it would be difficult for him to contact her. She should be more accessible, not closed behind a door.

Xena changed, her hands were trembling slightly with worry, but she recovered quickly. She left and began her walk past the cafe again. There, everyone looked at her without even hiding their interest. Xena ignored them this time and continued towards the main street. Some people stopped to talk to her, asked her how she was, was she was coming back permanently? Did she know anything about Ivan's murder? They asked many other questions. She did not give precise answers. She had been taught how to avoid questions, and answered with questions of her own.

Xena walked around part of her old neighbourhood but didn't stop at her house, although she wanted to. She remembered Danny's words and followed the route so she turned. She expected Long One or one of his men to appear from somewhere but nothing like that happened. Xena returned to the hotel tired of the attention from the people around her. She closed the door and leaned back on the bed. Xena hoped their plan would work and she wouldn't have to stay locked up here for long.

There was a knock on the door. It was the familiar signal and she invited Danny in.

'You look tired,' he said.

'Yes, I thought it would be easier but all these curious people with their thousands of questions…'

'I'm sorry,' he said sympathetically and sat down on the only chair in her room.

'Will he call?' she asked Danny.

'I don't know, Xena. People like Long One are unpredictable. He could call today or he might study you for a few days.'

Danny apparently thought like she did. It could be a long wait.

'What do we do now?' she asked.

'We'll wait. I will be with you all the time. My colleagues will watch what is happening around the town.'

Before Xena hadn't minded being with him, but now the tension between them was killing her. She sensed his presence even if she was in the other room or if she had her back to him. She didn't know how to deal with that feeling. She wanted to run away or worse, go and hug him. However, that would be a mistake and she knew it. She saw in his eyes that he felt the same way.

'We'll handle it,' he told her.

'Yes, I know,' she said, burying herself in the book she had begun to read. He looked away from her and stared out the window. The sun was hidden behind one of the mountain tops. He knew that it would rise again, and hide at the next peak, and so on several times a day at this time of year. In the summer, this changed because the sun rose high, above the peaks and hid only when it set in the west. Their hometown was really beautiful, but some people in it were rotten apples.

'What are you thinking about?' Xena asked him.

'The people of this town.'

'Which people exactly?'

'Everyone.'

Xena didn't ask him any more questions. She let him look out the window and she pretended to read a book. In fact, she kept looking at her phone or at Danny. She expected Long One to contact her somehow and waiting killed her. She couldn't wait. She was not like Danny. He seemed to be able to wait for days. However, she was more impatient. Xena snorted reluctantly and that caught his attention.

He looked at her questioningly.

'I just can't stand and do nothing.'

'What do you want to do? We can play cards, chess or go to the gym.'

She considered his proposal and chose the gym. He let her get ready and told her to go alone. He would go before her to check to make sure there were no strangers and ask her not to show that they knew each other.

It took Xena fifteen minutes to change and get better. She went downstairs to the gym, and found Danny running on one of the treadmills. She got on the exercise cycle, and started pedalling. Only the two of them were in the gym. Neither of them spoke for a while, each carried on with their training.

'You didn't tell me how the walk went?' his voice startled her.

'Alright. Many people stopped me and asked me questions. They asked me if I knew about Ivan's death. It was embarrassing but other than that, it was nice to see the town again. Have you walked down the main street recently?'

'Yes, the last time was a few months ago.'

'Do people recognise you?' she asked him.

'No. I was in uniform and questioning witnesses. Even my neighbour Elena didn't recognise me.'

Xena smiled. Elena was one of the gossips in the neighbourhood. Danny had really changed a lot. She stared at him. He felt her gaze and turned. Their eyes met and lingered for a while. Then they both stopped to look at each other. Xena moved to another piece of equipment, as far away from him as possible. At that moment, the gym door opened and two young men entered into a conversation. They argued about football. Xena didn't greet them but continued to do the exercises as if they were not there. Danny just nodded to them and kept running. A few minutes later, the gym was full of people and Danny gave her a faint sign that they had to leave.

He left the gym first waiting for her in the hallway and pretending to wipe his sweat with a towel. Xena walked past him like a stranger and picked up the elevator. He climbed the stairs. She was already in her room when he went up to the third floor. Danny hesitated about which room to go to hers or his but turned to his. He didn't want to be with her when she took a shower, it would kill him slowly. He entered his room and Billy and Ivanov were waiting for him. They had to discuss the plan for the next day. This would distract his thoughts from Xena and her naked body in the shower, he thought.

'You don't look well, Danny,' Billy said. 'You look tired. Do you want to take a day off?'

'No. I will manage, I will sleep tonight.'

The two men said nothing. They just looked at each other. Their experience suggested that it wasn't just the lack of sleep that made him tired. For Danny, this case was very personal and everyone knew it from the beginning. His fascination with Xena, which was obvious to everyone, even their bosses made his task even more difficult. Ivanov even considered removing him from the case but he knew that Xena trusted Danny and felt safe only around him and that stopped him from removing his friend. Without Danny Xena wouldn't have agreed to do anything. She would have returned to Britain on the first flight, Ivanov was sure of that. Now he could only pray that everything went according to plan and well. He thought that if they had to stay more than a week, Xena and Danny certainly wouldn't last that long. The feelings between them would flare up one way or another and then only God could help them. Ivanov was trying to be tactful, but Billy wasn't.

'For God's sake, Danny, don't stare at Xena like that all the time. Even I can tell through the cameras that there is something between you both and if I was next to you it would be even more obvious.'

'She was staring at me,' Danny tried to defend himself.

'Then don't look back at her and one piece of advice from me, don't kiss her. No matter how much you want to. If you kiss her, it's the end.'

'Do you say that from personal experience?' Danny asked him. Billy had met his wife in a similar situation. They were still very much in love, but Billy thought it had been simple luck that it had gone that way. Now he was trying to keep Danny from making a mistake and distracting himself. Any distraction in their work could cost someone's life. In this case, Xena's.

'Yes, I tell you from personal experience. Watch but don't touch. That is my advice.'

Danny sighed. It was easy for Billy to say. It was torture for Danny to stay close to Xena. He forced himself not to think of her as a woman, but as a witness. He had worked with women dozens of times without being emotionally attached. The problem was that she amazed and impressed him even before he spoke to her in London. This woman got under his skin long before he met her for the second time in his life and his interest in her was a long process and was no surprise. What surprised him was her interest in him.

Everyone had expected Long One to try to contact Xena or send one of his men but in the days that followed it never happened. The wait made Xena nervous. She wanted to provoke the bastard but the others wouldn't let her.

'Don't twist the lion's tail,' Ivanov told her. 'You don't even know half the evils this man has done.'

Xena took his advice but her nerves were strained. She would get up every morning, do her morning jogging and then work out with Danny at the gym or play cards. In those few days they became even closer. They were almost inseparable. However, Xena couldn't relax. In a few days she had visibly lost weight and stopped talking. Sometimes Danny saw the trembling of her hands and worried that she wouldn't be able to bear it mentally. One day he took her hands as they trembled.

'You need to calm down,' he told her. Then he stroked her cheek gently. She looked up at him and cried. Danny hugged her and tried to calm her. However, her closeness made him nervous. He forced himself away from her and went into the team room.

'The situation isn't good, is it?' Billy asked.

'No, it's not. I can't stand being that close to her, Billy. I can't concentrate when I'm in the same room with her.'

There was bitterness in his voice. His job was to keep her safe, not upset her. He knew that part of her psychological breakdown came from him. Danny took some mint drops and a glass of water and went to Xena again.

'Drink this, I hope it helps you calm down.'

She took the glass, drank and looked at him desperately.

'What are we going to do, Danny?' she asked him.

'We'll wait, but I think it's best to part company with you for a while.'

She was surprised by what he said, but she agreed. She knew he was right.

'I'll be around,' he said.

'Where?'

'In my room.'

'Alright,' she said but her eyes were sad.

'Only for a day or two. We both need a break, you know from...' he didn't go on, but she understood.

The next two days were very painful for Xena. She was alone everywhere, running, training and eating alone. Instead of reassuring her it made her even more nervous. She paced nervously in the room, her hands trembling more and more. She didn't feel protected when Danny wasn't around. She knew she was being watched all the time. Billy had told her he had even put cameras in her room and advised her to change in the bathroom. She knew she was not alone, but she was lonely and scared. She was afraid that Long One would reach her and at the same time she missed Danny very much. Xena guessed that the strange situation they were in made their feelings stronger. Perhaps in other circumstances the tension between them would not have been so. Yet, two strong feelings controlled her at the moment, fear and love. Her inability to deal with them made her vulnerable.

In the next room, Danny watched her walk nervously around her room, her hands were clasped tightly. Xena was wearing a sports vest and shorts. Her body was tight and graceful. It was hard for him to look at her like that. He wanted to go to her, hug her and reassure her, but he knew the idea wasn't good. Danny hoped Long One would get involved soon and he and everyone else could focus on other things, but Long One didn't. Xena's presence in the town obviously didn't bother him. Or he was thinking of something. The second thought drove Danny crazy. He couldn't imagine for a moment that something bad could happen to Xena. She had already had enough. Although she was upset and nervous, she did not give up. Many people in her place would have long ago packed their bags and left the town. That was one of the things that attracted him to her, she didn't give up. Danny was sure she already had a plan in her head to get out if she had to and he had one too. He stared at the screen again, Xena was still pacing the room.

An hour later Ivanov joined Danny.

'She is like a wildcat,' said the older man. 'Don't be fooled by the trembling of her hands, I know several women like her. In a tense situation she will cope. Now, however, she needs to calm down a bit.'

'I don't know what to do to calm her down.'

'I'll order some good food tonight. Bring it to her and talk to her. Try to calm her down and keep your hands away from her. I know you like her but a love affair will only complicate matters.'

Danny nodded and continued to watch Xena. He had to come up with something and calm her down.

At half-past-six, the food arrived and Danny knocked on the door of her room. She slowed before opening and was visibly surprised at the plates of food he was carrying.

'I thought you didn't want to see me again,' she told him.

'I didn't say such a thing. I said it would be good to rest for a while.'

Xena took the food from his hands and placed it on the small table. He pulled the table to her bed and Danny sat in the chair.

'What do you think will happen tonight?' Billy asked in the other room. He looked angrily at Ivanov. He didn't like his friend's plan at all.

'I hope Danny finds a way to calm her down,' Ivanov said.

'And Danny? Who's going to take care of his nerves?' Billy raised his voice slightly. 'I have found myself in such a situation and I don't recommend it even to the people I hate.'

'Danny will do,' Ivanov said. He watched what was happening in the other room. Cameras had been installed but they had agreed that there would be no sound. Xena deserved at least that personal space.

'Dream on,' Billy muttered. He was angry with both Ivanov and himself for agreeing to this. They had to find a way to challenge Long One, not experiment with Danny and Xena's feelings.

In the next room the two ate in silence. Xena divided the food into small pieces and hardly ate. The food was delicious but she wasn't hungry.

'You have to eat,' Danny said.

'I know, but I can't swallow and I'm not hungry.'

Dinner didn't go the way Danny had expected. Xena was closed in on herself, not talking, not eating, just rummaging on her plate. Finally, she simply moved it away, took a glass of water and sat down to watch him eat. Danny ate a little more and moved the plate aside as well. He had lost his appetite. He knew neither what to say nor what to do. He looked at her, picked up the plates and left the room. He sighed heavily as soon as he closed the door.

Xena was clutching a glass of water. She tried to calm down, but she couldn't. She decided to take a shower, it always helped her. She went into the bathroom, turned on the hot water and let it run down her body. She stayed in the bathroom for almost an hour. However, the shower didn't help her. She got dressed, went back to bed, and curled up. Tears streamed from her eyes, she tried to stop them but she couldn't.

In the other room, Danny was watching her. He watched her cry and his heart sank. Xena's body began to shake with tears.

Danny couldn't stand it and went to her. He sat on the bed. She didn't turn around, she didn't send him away, just kept crying. Danny looked at her then took her hand and tried to calm her. Her crying passed slowly.

'I'm better,' she told him.

'No, you're not,' he said softly. 'You got involved in this situation and now I am very sorry about that.'

She said nothing, got up and went to the bathroom to wash her face. He moved to his chair and waited for her to come out.

'Come here,' he told her as she walked past him and pulled her into his lap. Xena didn't resist, on the contrary, she hugged him. She liked his warmth.

He pulled her closer to him and kissed her hair. It felt good. Her hair smelled of flowers. A slight pleasant smell. Xena had her head resting on his shoulder. He couldn't see her face, the room was almost dark. He kissed her hair again, brushed it lightly and stroked her neck gently, kissing the spot where his hand had passed. Xena moved her head slowly and looked into his eyes. Danny leaned down to kiss her gently touching her lips. She didn't resist, she pulled him closer to her. Danny's arms wrapped around her waist. He had already lost control. He put one hand under her tank top and stroked the skin of her belly. Xena sighed.

'Should I stop?' Danny asked her.

'No,' she whispered softly in his ear. She kissed his neck and continued with gentle kisses down to his chest. Danny continued to examine her body with his hands, while trying to keep both of them stable in the chair. His hand wrapped around one of her breasts. Xena sighed as he touched her. His other hand aimed at her panties. He expected her to push him away but instead she settled more comfortably and spread her legs slightly. There were slight moans from her and he was no longer in control. Danny made her get up and moved her to the bed. They continued their love game there for a short time and then made love. When they were done, Xena curled up in a ball and Danny hugged her. They fell asleep for a short time, then made love again. In the end, they were so exhausted that they simply relaxed next to each other and fell into a deep sleep.

Danny woke up to a noise in the bathroom. The water was flowing and from what he heard, Xena was crying again. He got up quickly, opened the door and found her sitting under the running water. Xena was crying, she then got up, went over to the toilet and started vomiting. Danny stood beside her and hugged her tightly.

He had seen several people in a similar condition. The stress turned people's stomachs upside down. This was happening to her now. She would feel better in the morning but she didn't know it. When Xena stopped vomiting and went back to the hot shower Danny followed her, put her on his lap and began to soothe her. A few minutes later Xena calmed down and they went back to bed. They fell asleep almost instantly. Xena's breathing was calm this time, there was no sign of her nervousness. With Danny behind her she felt calm and safe.

In the morning she woke up first. She kissed him on the cheek, got dressed and went on her usual morning jogging. Danny went back to his room, changed and joined Billy and Ivanov to watch her on camera.

'I told you not to kiss her,' Billy scolded.

'Do you have any idea what you're doing?' Ivanov shouted at him.

Danny didn't answer. He didn't know what to say. He didn't regret what had happened between him and Xena. He would not excuse himself or give an explanation because he couldn't.

'You know I have to inform management now,' Ivanov kept shouting. 'Shit, Danny. Why didn't you keep your hands off her?'

'Because she needed me and I needed her,' Danny said in the end.

The men argued for a while and watched Xena run.

As she ran, Xena thought about the night she'd spent with Danny. The feeling of being with him was great. She now understood that she had only had sex with Ivan, but it was different with Danny. He gave himself to her in the same way she did to him. He made love to her, it was a whole new experience for her and she was worried about how long this would last. Xena looked at the people in the cafe and decided that she felt more confident now and had to take action. She finished her last sprint and headed straight for the cafe. She would go and leave a message for Long One.

Xena entered the small coffee-scented room and to her surprise Adi was standing at the bar. The two women looked at each other for a while. Adi was visibly nervous about Xena's presence.

'Hi!' Xena greeted her.

'Hi,' Adi said nervously. She kept looking at Xena with obvious concern.

'I know about you and Ivan. I didn't come for that. I want you to send a message to Long One.'

'What message?' her ex-friend asked.

'Tell him I have something he cares about.'

Xena picked up a napkin from the counter, asked for a pen and wrote down her phone number.

'Okay, I'll try to tell him what you said.'

Xena turned to leave and just then she heard a child's voice.

'Mum, look,' it said, looking Xena in the eye. Xena took a step back. The boy was a small copy of Ivan. Eyes, nose and chin, as well as slightly pouty lips.

Adi pushed him behind her. The eyes of the two women met, Xena staring, as furious as she had ever looked in her life.

'Did you see what you did with your actions?' Adi told her, 'leaving a child without a father.'

'And another was killed before it was born,' Xena told her, seeing the shock in her ex-friend's eyes.

Xena left the cafe furious. The onlookers present at the quarrel made her a quick place and she passed them without paying attention to them.

She entered the hotel and instead of boarding the elevator, climbed the stairs to the third floor in one breath.

Danny, Billy and Ivanov had watched her enter the cafe. They saw something happening but they didn't know what. Danny was furious with her. Why did she risk going there?

He entered her room immediately after her.

'What the hell are you doing?'

'Did you know about the child?' she asked him directly. Her eyes glared at him.

He nodded.

'Why didn't you tell me?' she rebuked him.

'I wanted to, but I saw how you reacted when you found out about Ivan and Adi. I was looking for a good time to tell you about the boy.'

She glared at him and sat on the bed.

'How can I trust you if you're going to hide such things from me?' she asked him.

'Okay, let me explain. I'll order a small breakfast and coffee and explain why I didn't tell you.'

'I hope you have a good explanation,' she said.

He ignored her, turned and just before he opened the door, he asked her, 'Why did you go there?'

'I left a message for Long One. I told him I had something for him and left him my phone number.'

He gasped slightly. A cunning move, he thought, but he didn't tell her that. He had to warn Billy and Ivanov to expect inclusion.

Ten minutes later he returned to Xena with a few croissants and coffee. He left them on the table and made her eat.

'I'm listening,' Xena reminded him. She sipped her coffee, took a bite of the croissant and waited for his explanation. She was calmer now.

'When I was fourteen years old I found out that I had a half-sister.'

This time Xena gasped in surprise.

'She was exactly the same age as this boy. I was furious with everyone then. My father, my mother, my father's mistress, and most of all my little sister. She had his eyes. It couldn't be mistaken who the father was.'

'I'm sorry. I didn't know.'

'I experienced it hard. Since then, I haven't spoken to my father and my mother. I also moved away. However, the good thing is that my brother and I finally decided that our sister had done nothing wrong and now we are very close to her. Few people know that we are her brothers, most think that we are cousins.'

Xena didn't know what to say. She set the croissant on her plate and stroked his hand lightly.

'I knew it would hurt you deeply, so I didn't tell you,' he said.

'I understand. I'm sorry for what you went through.'

'It's over now,' he smiled. 'And when this is all over, I want to introduce you to her.'

'I'll be glad to see her.'

This again raised the silent question of what would happen to them in the future. Danny pulled her close and kissed her.

'What's your sister's name?' she asked him.

'Laura,' he said. 'She's grown up now. I can't believe how fast she's grown. Eat now, you need strength. Then we'll go to Billy and Ivanov to discuss what we're going to do when Long One calls you.'

Just then, Xena phone rang.

'Pick it up after the third ring,' Danny told her, staring at the phone number that was ringing.

'Hello,' Xena said.

'You were looking for me,' Long One said.

'I have something of yours.'

'Right? And what is it?'

'Something from the river.'

He was silent.

'I want proof, a photo or just bring what you have.'

'I'm not that stupid,' Xena said. 'I won't bring what I have. I just will bring proof that I have it.'

'All right. Tonight at six in my pizzeria.'

'No, that will not happen. We will see each other at that time but in another place. In Mitko's pub.'

Long One was silent for a while, then agreed.

Xena hung up.

'You did well,' Danny told her.

'But now I must quickly figure out what to give him as proof.'

'Don't worry about it. We found your bloodied and wet clothes in Dora's house. We can use them and if you give us a good description of the wooden stick you fought with and which we assume he beat Ivan with, we will take a fake photo, as if you own it.'

'All right,' Xena said. There was nervousness in her voice. Things were starting to happen.

Xena spent the whole day mentally preparing for her meeting with Long One. At about four o'clock, when she and Billy were alone in the room, he called her and postponed the meeting for the next day.

'He's trying to figure out what you have,' Billy told her. 'He is probably questioning his people from the police and since he didn't understand anything in particular, he is trying to gain some time. You have to be careful tomorrow when you run Xena. This man is capable of anything to save himself.'

She nodded. Billy looked at her and said, 'Danny is a very good boy.'

'I know.'

'He would do anything for you. It's not easy for him after what happened to his grandparents. If something happens to you he will die you know...'

'I know. What happened to his grandparents?' Xena asked. She thought they had died a natural death.

'I thought you knew,' Billy said. 'Didn't Danny tell you?'

'No.'

Danny and Ivanov entered the room and interrupted their conversation. The four discussed what to do in the morning.

Half an hour later Xena returned to her room. She opened the balcony, and breathed in the fresh air. She needed that view. She was looking at the mountain and thinking about Danny. There was something sad about him and something personal about this whole case. She had felt it when they first spoke at the Embassy. Now she knew something about what it was, but she wanted to know exactly what had happened to his grandparents and what Long One's involvement was.

Danny entered the room after a short warning knock on the door. He didn't want to startle her. He didn't approach her because he didn't want anyone to see them together, so as not to destroy the illusion that she was alone. She stood looking at the mountain for a while longer and then finally turned and looked at him. There was concern in her eyes.

'Will you tell me about your grandparents?'

'Yes, Billy mentioned to me that he told you.'

Danny sat down in his chair and stared at the carpet on the floor, his gaze drifting.

'The story is similar to Ivan's. Grandpa borrowed money from Long One so he could pay for firewood for the winter. I don't know if you know, but Long One's interest rates are very high.'

'I know,' Xena said softly.

'He failed to return the money on time. He didn't tell my grandmother and my father so as not to bother them. In the end, however, he confessed to them. Long One threatened to kidnap me and my brother. My parents and grandmother tried to collect the money but managed to pay him only in part. Ten percent of the loan remained unpaid. To make sure that nothing would happen to the both of us our parents made a decision and we moved to live in Sofia overnight. Two weeks later, Grandma found Grandpa dead, poisoned. She died shortly after.'

Danny looked away from the carpet and looked Xena in the eye.

'I couldn't wait to catch him since then, Xena. You are the only chance for people like us to catch him and judge him for what he has done to so many people. Do you understand how important this is, not only for you and me, but for the people in this town?'

'I understand. And this between us?' she asked.

'It's just between you and me. I didn't plan it, if that's what you're asking me.'

Deeply in her soul, Xena knew that was the truth. Danny wouldn't take advantage of her, he wasn't that kind of person. Not that she was a specialist in knowing people. Ivan and Adi's child was good proof of that.

Xena sat on Danny's lap. He hugged her and kissed her neck.

'I'm sorry. I should have told you earlier but my problems were nothing compared to yours and your experience cannot be compared to anything. I have my family, my job and my friends. While you had to run and hide alone. I didn't want to burden you.'

'You should have told me,' she whispered softly.

'I should have.' Danny hugged her even tighter. He turned her over and kissed her.

They moved to the bed and made love again. Danny just couldn't be away from her. This woman had enchanted him. He would never have allowed himself to sleep with a woman during an action before. However, it couldn't be controlled. He hugged her again and they both fell asleep. Short but healthy sleep. They both woke up to the sound of someone knocking on the wall. Danny dressed quickly and went to the next room.

'One of Long One's men just walked into the hotel. Warn Xena not to open the door to anyone.'

Danny went to warn her, made her walk away from the door and not stand near the window.

He himself returned to his room. He was watching Long One's man. He knew him, his name was Miro. He was one of the people gathering information for Long One. Danny calmed down. The man talked to the hotel staff for a while then left.

'Long One sent Miro to inquire about you,' he informed Xena.

'I got his attention.'

'Yes.' Danny knew Xena had aimed at him. That scared him. He didn't want to lose her.

'Do you want to have dinner?' he asked her.

'Yes, I'm starving,' she said, clutching her stomach.

Danny followed her gesture and wished he could take her to bed again. For now, however, he had to focus on her safety. Sex only distracted them. They both had to be alert, despite the cameras, Danny worried that someone might enter her room and kill her.

'I'll stay with you tonight.'

'Alright,' she agreed. She hadn't expected to be alone.

Danny returned with food packages half an hour later. They ate in silence but this time there was no tension between them. Rather a tacit understanding. Xena took a shower and so did Danny, then they laid down in each other's arms and fell asleep.

Danny had woken up at midnight. He was standing by the window watching what was happening outside. He stayed there until morning. From time to time he turned his gaze to the sleeping Xena. Her breathing was even now. She slept peacefully. It made him feel better.

Xena woke up just in time for her morning jogging. She saw Danny on the chair. He had probably been there all night. He looked tired and worried.

'Did something happen while I was sleeping?' she asked him.

'No,' he said. 'Everything was calm.'

He pulled her close to him and kissed her. She laughed.

'It's weird,' she said and this time she pulled him up and kissed him.

'That's right,' he smiled. 'Get ready now, because you'll be late.'

Xena got ready and went for a run. The air outside was unusually cold. She was dripping lightly. It reminded her of the day she last saw Ivan. The fact that he and Adi had a child really shocked her. She had accepted his infidelity but the child changed her feelings. That what had been between him and Adi was not just one of Adi's whims as Xena had thought earlier. It had been stronger. Adi changed men often and knew how to avoid getting pregnant. Apparently, things with Ivan got so out of control that they had a child as a result. Xena knew her ex-friend well, and now she felt sorry for Adi who was left alone with her child and could not hide who the father was. The town would not forgive her for taking another woman's boyfriend, and that he had been killed because of her was certainly no longer a secret.

Running Xena decided it was best not to dig into those wounds and she would try not to meet Adi again. They had nothing more to say to each other. The only thing that already connected them was the tragedy that had happened to the man they both loved at the same time. Another question was which of them had truly loved Ivan. There was no doubt in Xena's mind that she had not been in his last thoughts.

She stared at the cafe and wondered if Adi was there today. The stadium was still empty. The rain intensified and forced Xena to return to the hotel earlier than planned. Shortly after she returned her phone rang. She waited until the third ring, as Danny had recommended and picked it up. It was Long One.

'I'll be waiting for you in half an hour in the cafe. Bring the proof with you.'

'Nope. It will not happen. The meeting for tonight remains. If you want, come, if you don't want to, don't. You decide,' and Xena interrupted the conversation.

That's my girl, Danny thought after listening in on the conversation. She doesn't leave Long One any choice.

'She's good,' Billy smiled.

'If she hadn't been good, she wouldn't be alive now,' Ivanov said. 'It wasn't a coincidence that it took us so long to find her and I guess she was kind of waiting for us at the Embassy too.'

Danny had had that thought too. He was almost certain she expected to see him there.

He took breakfast and coffee and joined her in the room.

'You did well,' he told her.

'Thanks. I'm not sure that when he's in front of me I'll behave so well.'

'You'll be fine, I'm sure and don't forget that even if you don't see us, we will be with you.'

They had breakfast, drank their coffee and moved into Ivanov and Billy's room. They showed her what they had done quickly as evidence. The plan was for Xena to show it to Long One and convince him that the proof was somewhere around. The trick was to ask him for money in exchange for some of it. Time would tell if that would work.

Xena dined alone in her room. She tried to concentrate again, so she opened the balcony door and stared at the rain. It was raining hard, the sound of drops falling on the leaves of the trees was noisy but soothing. The terrace was filled with water but it was quickly draining from the small gutter made especially for this purpose. As soon as the rain stopped, a fog descended. The fog rose from the ground and rose slowly up the mountain. It reminded Xena of one of the songs her grandmother often sang to her. The song mentioned exactly that moment when the fog engulfs the mountain and when the mountain engulfs the fog. It was difficult to say which of the two statements was true but the view was impressive.

In the afternoon the sun appeared briefly but then it began to rain again.

Xena prepared for the meeting with Long One. She was calm, there was no sign of nervousness. She left five minutes before the meeting hour and waited. A slight tickle on her back made her think someone was watching her. It could be anyone, one of the people of Long One or someone from the investigation team. Xena ordered coffee and water but didn't drink from them. Danny's account of his poisoned grandfather had warned her to expect anything from this man. Long One was late but Xena sat still and waited.

'You've become very brave,' his voice startled behind her.

'Sometimes you have no choice,' she told him. She was a little nervous when she met his eyes but she tried to look calm.

He sat across from her, ordered a beer and looked at her.

'I don't have all day, so show me what you got,' he said rudely.

He looked at her phone like a child waiting for his toy. Xena picked up her phone, found the pictures she needed and showed them to him. She gripped the phone tightly, showing him she wouldn't let him pick it up.

'We both know what that is, I don't need to mention it. I guess you also know whose DNA is there.'

Long One glared at her. He looked sinister in his anger.

'Where did you get this?'

'Does it matter where? You tried to kill me.'

Xena looked at him with obvious disgust. He looked at her with his small eyes. His look was cold and angry. Apparently, he couldn't forgive himself for missing her then.

'But you're a witch and you survived.' Long One lost his temper. He saw the satisfaction on her face and looked at her with an even more vicious look. 'What do you want?'

'I want a million. That's how much I value my life and the life of my child at that moment. If you think thats small, I'll add a sum for its father's life.'

'Bitch.' He spat on her. Few people looked at them but even those who did looked away quickly at the sight of Long One.

'Yes, I'm learning fast,' Xena told him. She put her hands under the table so he wouldn't know they were shaking.

'If you don't pay me by noon tomorrow, I'll turn it over to the police. Not the police here,' she laughed,' but the District Police. I understand that they were looking for witnesses and evidence.'

Long One looked at her cruelly; it made her feel sick, but Xena overcame those feelings and forced herself to stay calm. She had been told that this would frighten and infuriate him at the same time.

'Bitch,' he repeated.

'Bastard,' she said losing her temper. 'Tomorrow at noon here. If you don't come or if something happens to me the evidence of Ivan's murder will go where it needs to go and then you'll know what it's like to run or you'll know how wide a prison cell is. It's not like you have no choice.'

Xena got up quickly without paying her bill and walked to the hotel. She could feel many eyes on her. Her breathing quickened, she couldn't wait to go to her room and wash the smell away from her. Danny was waiting for her there and so was Ivanov.

'You managed to get him out of his skin. So far we have a confession of attempted murder. For your murder.'

Xena smiled slightly.

'I'm sorry, but if you didn't notice, he spat on me. I need a long shower.'

'That's why we're here. We need his DNA,' Danny told her. 'You managed to kill two rabbits with one bullet today.'

He took out gloves and test tubes and took a sample from her face. Xena slipped into the bathroom immediately afterward and as promised, stayed there for almost an hour. She rubbed her face with everything possible. She wanted to get rid of the smell of that scumbag.

Finally she calmed down and left. Danny was waiting for her with dinner.

'I thought you were going to be hungry.'

She was hungry and looked at him lustfully.

'We can quench that hunger later. Now you need real food.'

Xena sat down next to him and they ate in silence.

'I wanted to take a knife from the table and kill him when he spat on me,' she admitted.

'If it was me, I'd have wanted the same thing.'

'Will we catch him tomorrow, Danny?'

'I hope so, but he's more likely to recover from the shock today and try to do something to you tomorrow. So eat and go to bed. I will stay with you tonight, we will have to sleep to gather strength for the battle.'

'Do you think it won't be easy to surrender?'

'I'm sure,' he replied seriously, adding, 'I'll sleep with you but you must know something. Two more people will come along just in case. The government wants to protect you after today's confession. Everyone is convinced that Long One will try to kill you, if not tonight, then tomorrow before or during your meeting.'

'What do you think?' she asked him.

He walked over to her and kissed her.

'I don't even dare to think about it. It's too personal for me and I don't think sober. So I did what I had to do. I called for reinforcement.'

She nodded understandingly. She understood his hint, they shouldn't indulge in caresses. It was best to lie down and sleep. Several people were guarding them, they would warn them if danger arose.

Xena woke up early in the morning. Danny was gone, apparently out without her noticing. It was too early for jogging, so she just opened the terrace and watched the sunrise. She was worried about what would happen today. She was convinced that many people would watch and guard her but she already knew that Long One had a wealth of experience in killing people who interfered with him. This could be the last sunrise she saw.

Xena remembered that when Ivan said that Long One would kill him, she didn't believe him. She hadn't heard of any murders in the town but now she knew he had successfully covered them up. He paid the right people to close their eyes. How many mothers had lost their children and how many children had lost their parents? The phone alarm took her out of her thoughts. Xena dressed quickly, wondered where Danny was but he came to her just before she left. He hugged her and looked into her eyes.

'Some of Long One's people are around. Be very careful, even at the slightest sign of danger return to the hotel.'

She nodded and whispered, 'I'm scared.'

'Fear will keep you safe and remember, I will follow your every step. We have a tracking device in your trainers, so we will literally know about every step you take.'

Danny kissed her hair. He had a bad feeling and he didn't seem to want to let her go but she slowly pulled away from his embrace and left the room.

Xena started running slowly. The red pavement was soaked with water, puddles had formed in places and she had to either go around them or jump over them. She decided that she would run fifteen minutes shorter, just in case. She ran evenly and counted. At the same time, she tried to look around for something unusual but saw nothing suspicious. The air was cool, there were no people in the cafe yet but light was leaking from the windows, which meant there was someone inside. Probably her ex-friend Adi, Xena thought. She kept running, saw something fly by and just for a split second before she took the next step something knocked her to the ground. Xena tried to free herself but failed. She was like a fish in a net, although she could not see the net. Someone went behind her and hit her on the head. Xena felt a sharp pain but before she could react and try to defend herself someone hit her on the head again which stunned her and she fainted.

There was a commotion in the hotel in the rooms of the investigation team. No one could figure out what had happened. They saw Xena fall and then a man in camouflage clothes pulled her out of the stadium. Several people ran there but when they got to the place there was no one. Xena was gone.

Danny had the feeling that someone had hit him with a hammer. He couldn't believe they had caught her. At first, he couldn't react, then he started shouting for more light. He looked around the place where Xena had fallen and saw small, very fine marks. He immediately understood how she had been caught. She had been literally caught in a fishing net entangled in a fishing line. The kind that local fishermen used when the river was stormy.

Through the earpiece, he was told where Xena was. They had tracked her with the devices they had put in her shoes. Xena and her captors were travelling out of town, according to what the tracker showed.

Danny and the two newcomers to their team got in a car and drove off after the signal. They had a man guarding the way out of the town and they called him to stop the traffic so that no one couldn't take Xena out of the city. The tracker indicated that Xena was in an abandoned factory.

Danny called a few more men for reinforcement and slowly entered the factory with the car's headlights off. The factory was built just below the mountain, so it was still dark all around. The sun's rays would shine on it much later than the rest of the town. There was cool air inside; stagnant air that froze the bones. The iron window frames were rusty, and everything was covered with thick dust. There was no indication that there were people in this building. Danny and his two colleagues parted ways and began searching everywhere. There was complete silence, no sign of Xena or the man who abducted her. Danny went to the place where he was handing over the tracker and found Xena's clothes and trainers. She had been stripped as a precaution. Danny called for no more people to come. His heart stopped for a moment. He was now certain that they didn't know where Xena was and if Long One knew that the investigation team was on his heels, he would kill her immediately. So, Danny called his men quietly, left Xena's clothes and trainers where they were and left the factory as quietly as possible. They had to find another way to find her as soon as possible.

Danny and his men returned to the hotel and watched the recording of Xena's abduction.

'There must be something! Watch carefully,' Ivanov said.

They watched the recording three times. The third time Danny asked them to stop the screen on the man who kidnapped Xena. Then he followed his movements slowly and recognised him. Xena and Danny talked about him a few days ago. One of their childhood friends was one of Long One's men. Xena had told Danny about him and now, seeing the man's gait and crooked left leg, he recognised him.

'His name is Anton. He lives in the upper part of the town, near Xena's house.'

Two of his men immediately headed there and Billy traced his phone. To everyone's surprise, Anton was at Xena's house.

'There is logic to this plan,' Ivanov said. 'Obviously, Long One thinks the evidence is there.'

The day they had arrived in Vedna, Billy had put cameras in Xena's house in case she decided to stop by. He turned on the cameras and they saw her. She was naked, tied to one of the heating pipes. It was impossible to see if she was conscious or not. Anton couldn't be seen. Danny hurried out of the room. He had to get to Xena as soon as possible. Ivanov went with him.

'Xena has company. Long One has just joined her,' Billy shouted.

'I'm going to kill him,' Danny said through gritted teeth.

Xena regained consciousness when someone splashed water on her face. Long One stood opposite her and looked at her.

'Where are they?' he asked, leaning over her, and looking into her eyes.

Xena was silent. She looked around and saw that they were in her home. She was cold and realized that she was naked. She tried to cover herself. Only then did she find that she had been tied to a pipe.

'This time I decided not to leave any evidence,' he grinned when he saw the worry of her nakedness.

'Where is it? We don't have all day. You think I don't know you're not alone? I give you five minutes to tell me where the evidence is or who has it.'

She didn't answer. Long One slapped her with the back of his hand. Xena moaned in cold and pain but said nothing. She hoped someone would come soon and get her out of here. Then she remembered that they had undressed her, and Danny and his men probably didn't know where she is now.

Long One was in his element, cursing and hitting her several times.

'I will kill you like I did with your boyfriend. Your blood will run out and no one will come to your rescue.'

'They'll find the evidence and put you in prison,' Xena shouted.

'I won't leave any evidence this time. I will burn you alive if I have to.'

'If you do, the police will get the evidence and take you away for a long time.'

'They can't prove anything with the evidence alone.'

Xena saw Danny enter quietly. Long One was talking and hitting everything around and he didn't see him. Danny gestured for her to stay calm and to speak, pointing to his microphone.

Xena had to challenge Long One to confess, everything was being recorded.

'They will prove it. I wrote an exact description of what happened that night.'

'And what happened? You weren't there. You ran away, leaving your lover. You are so disloyal.' Long One grinned angrily.

'I found the wooden stick with which you beat him with, there is his and your DNA on it.'

'He's not the first person I've killed, you fool, and you won't be the last. With a little money, your rod and clothes will disappear. You better give the evidence to me now and I promise to kill you quickly and painlessly.'

'It won't happen,' Xena laughed at him. He swung to hit her, but Danny and one of his colleagues stopped him and knocked him to the ground. Long One didn't know where it all came from, then he looked at Danny and recognised him.

'Danny The Puppy. You became very brave, huh?'

Danny looked at Long One with regret, as though he wanted to beat him there on the spot. Instead, he smiled, picked up Long One and whispered loud enough that Xena could hear, 'I learned from a reliable source that although you are long, some important parts of your body are very short.'

Long One glared at him. At that moment more people entered the room. Danny handed them Long One and went to untie Xena. He found a blanket and wrapped it around her.

'It's over,' he told her and made the same gentle gesture typical of him, stroking her cheek with the back of his hand. Then he pulled back part of her hair and kissed her.

'I was worried I wouldn't find you,' he admitted.

'I know,' she said.

He helped her up on her feet and sit on the bed.

'How did you find me?'

'Do you remember telling me that Anton was one of Long One's men? I recognised him by his gait. We tracked his phone, and it took us here. Fortunately, Billy had set up cameras in case you decided to visit your house.'

'So, we were lucky.'

'Yes. It is all over now.'

'And I can go.'

Danny looked at her questioningly.

'Do you already have plans?' he asked.

'Yes. I'll tell you as soon as I get dressed and warm up.'

'Ivanov was right. You always have a plan,' he said, pulling her close to keep her warm.

Xena shivered. Danny helped her into one car, turned on the heating and drove her to the hotel with another of his colleagues. He was still worried about her. They didn't know how many people were involved and who else would want to harm her. When they arrived at the hotel, he accompanied her to her room and told her to rest. Danny still had work to do. He left a guard at her door and joined his colleagues who had begun making arrests of people who they knew they were involved in Long One's business.

Xena didn't see Danny until late at night. She tried to leave the room, but the man guarding her asked her not to leave. Xena dined alone, missing Danny's company. She began to wonder what would happen to them both. They hadn't discussed it. They hadn't discussed their feelings or their plans, but they had to do it and Xena didn't know what to tell him. She wanted to spend more time with him, but she knew what his job was, and he probably wouldn't have time for it.

Danny was thinking of Xena, too. After making all the arrests, they had to return to Sofia. He didn't know if she would want to go with him or if she wanted to stay in Vedna for a little longer.

'She's in your head again, isn't she?' Billy asked him.

'Yes. I don't know what to do from now on.'

'Don't wonder, go to her. After the experience today, she certainly needs you now. Ivanov and I will finish here. I will see you in Sofia tomorrow, right?'

'Yes, see you tomorrow.'

Danny went back to the hotel and knocked on Xena's door. She opened it for him. The two embraced and stood there for a while, clinging to each other.

'I was afraid you wouldn't find me.'

'I was afraid of that too, but I found you and now we're here.'

'What are we going to do?' she asked quietly.

'I don't know. What do you want us to do?'

'I want more time with you.'

'So, we want the same thing. I have to go home tonight. Do you want to come with me, or you prefer to stay here?'

'I don't want to stay here. I will come with you.'

'Well then. Gather your things and we'll go to my apartment.'

He hugged her again and kissed her.

'I couldn't believe someone took you away from me in just one second,' he told her. 'I was going to kill him. I hope it doesn't happen again.'

'It will not happen again. I promise,' she smiled slightly.

Xena tried not to think about what she had experienced during the day. Instead, she focused her efforts on packing. She definitely wouldn't miss the hotel and the town.

Ten minutes later, Xena and Danny left the hotel. They were just getting in the car when Xena saw Adi coming out of the cafe. She asked Danny to wait for her and headed for her ex-friend.

Adi stopped, tears streaming from her eyes.

'You caught him,' she said.

'We caught him,' Xena confirmed.

'Look, Xena. I'm sorry for everything. Things just got out of control with Ivan, and I didn't know how to tell you.'

Xena approached her and hugged the crying woman.

'I know. It just shouldn't have happened that way.'

'Will you come back here?' Adi asked her.

'No, I don't think so. I will return to the United Kingdom.'

'And your house?'

Deeply In The Soul

'I haven't thought about what I was going to do with my house. I will probably sell it.'

'You hate this town, huh?'

'I don't hate it. I just want to leave it in the past. It reminds me of things I don't want to remember. Maybe it's time for you to go somewhere with a fresh start too.'

'Maybe, but I'd rather not. I'm neither as smart nor as brave as you.'

Xena smiled. She was neither smarter nor braver than Adi. Life forced her to take risks and get smarter.

'Okay, I have to go.'

'I understand that Danny helped you.'

'Yes, me and Danny...' Xena did not finish.

'Who would have thought that you two would get together,' Adi said.

'Yes, it's a surprise even to me,' Xena laughed. 'Good luck, Adi.'

'Good luck to you too.'

Xena got back in the car and she and Danny headed for the capital.

'What did she tell you?' he asked her.

'She is relieved that Long One will be responsible for Ivan's murder and wondered what I would do from now on.'

'And what are you going to do from now on?' he asked her.

She laughed and asked, 'Do you like surfing?'

'I don't know, I've never surfed before.'

'Do you want to learn?'

'Why do you ask?'

'If they let you out of work for a few weeks we can go to Cornwall. I think we deserve a rest.'

Danny laughed. Xena kept astonishing him. Most people after an abduction needed to be left alone, to talk to a psychologist, to feel sorry for themself. She wanted to teach him to surf instead.

'I'll talk to my bosses. Even if they give me a few weeks off, it won't happen right away. It will take a few days.'

'No problem. It will give me time to see Gal and Dary.'

Danny looked at her.

'What?' she asked him.

'You know Gal is in love with you, don't you?'

Xena opened her mouth to say something, then closed it. Finally, she said, 'No, honestly, I thought we liked each other as friends. He is much younger than me.'

'I'm younger, too,' he laughed.

'Not so much.'

They both fell silent.

'Anyway, thank you for telling me. Now that I think about it, I realise you're right.'

'Just be careful not to hurt his feelings.'

'I promise. You seem to like him?'

'I do like him. While I was looking for you, I often stopped by to talk to him. I was hoping he would reveal exactly where you lived in London.'

'He didn't know. Nobody knew.'

'I know, but even if he knew, he wouldn't tell me. Anyway, we became friends. He promised to kill me if something bad happened to you or if I hurt you.'

Xena laughed out loud.

'Well, in that case, be careful not to hurt me.'

'I have no such intentions. Quite the opposite,' he said with a smile.

6

HOW LONG DOES HAPPINESS LAST?

They arrived at Danny's apartment just before midnight. His apartment was modestly furnished, and it was obvious that only he lived there. Not that Xena was expecting anything else, but her life had shown her many surprises recently, and anything was possible for her. For the next two days, Danny was busy with work and so that there would be no more surprises, Ivanov had provided her with security. It was not known what connections Long One had. According to some, he had promised a generous reward to the one who killed her, but Xena didn't know if that was true. The investigation team hadn't told her, but she wondered if they didn't want to scare her. She had done enough and now they had to protect her. No one wanted her to get hurt. First, because she was Danny's girlfriend, second because everyone liked her and third, she was a key witness in Long One's case and even if she didn't realise it, she was still a target.

Her decision to return to Britain, even for a short time, was welcome by all. Long One would not find her easily there and only Danny would know where she was, at least that was the hope.

Xena set aside one day just for Dary, and one day just for Gal. She wanted to see them undisturbed, with no other presence but her bodyguards.

Dary was in an advanced stage of pregnancy. She was expecting the baby at any moment and complained of low back and leg pain. She introduced Xena to the baby's father, a nice young man whom Xena liked from the first minute she met him. Dary was very tired, and Xena didn't stay long with her. She wanted to let her rest.

However, when she met Gal, they spent the whole day outside. They walked in the park and drank beer, something Xena had never done in her life before. They walked the main streets. Gal wanted to know all the details about her stay in Vedna.

'I was scared at times, but Danny was by my side.'

'I understand from your eyes that there is something more between you both.'

'That's right.' Xena laughed.

'He stole you from me.'

'Not so, I'm still yours, but as a friend and I hope to see you again very soon.'

'I'll come to you when you need me the most. Next time, I'll save you from the bad guy,' he joked.

'I hope I don't meet any more bad guys.'

'And I hope so too. What will you do now? Do you want to work in my nightclub? You know I'll always have a place for you there.'

'You'll probably be surprised, but I'm thinking of starting fresh and moving to Cornwall.'

'The heavenly place you keep telling me about. In that case, I will have to come and visit you there one day.'

'Of course, as soon as I am settled.'

She would miss Gal a lot, Xena was sure of that, but she didn't want to stay in Sofia for long. She wanted to go to the south of England as soon as possible and dive into the ocean.

Xena and Danny headed to Cornwall. Danny had managed to take three weeks off and they had packed two suitcases and taken a dream vacation. Lisa had recommended a place to stay for those three weeks. It was time out of reality. After that Xena had to find another place to live and start her new life.

For two weeks, Xena and Danny learned to surf, walked along the coast, and enjoyed each other. They had rented a house that was a ten-minute walk from the ocean. They ran to the beach in the morning, then had breakfast at one of the bars nearby. They liked to drink their coffee and watch the waves. The people around were friendly and smiling. Overall, this place was reassuring. They often stayed up late, lit a fire on the beach and talked to the people who joined them. The stress they were used to before was simply missing here.

'I understand why you want to live here,' Danny said one morning. 'I wish I could stay too.'

'It would be very nice if you could.'

'I have a contract for another three years at the agency, I can't just leave.'

'Then you can just come and see me when you can,' Xena suggested.

'You know it's not that easy for me.'

'I know it was just a suggestion.'

'You could come to visit me,' Danny offered.

'With pleasure, at least once every three months.'

'I don't want to put pressure on you, Xena. I just want to see you as often as possible.'

'I know. We'll find a way, won't we?'

'Yes. We will find a way. Then I would look for a job here after three years. You are right about this place. It is calm and relaxing here. I'll miss it. I'll miss you too.'

'I'm still here. We have a whole week and a half ahead of us. Let's postpone this conversation.'

'You're right,' Danny said and without her seeing him, he looked at her.

He wouldn't be able to leave her. With each passing day, it was getting worse. He thought of her and her new beginning here. He fully supported her choice, but he would not survive a week without seeing her and he knew it. He had to find a way to get rid of the agency contract or ask to be transferred here, which he knew was possible, but he didn't want to tell Xena until he knew for certain. In any case, he had to return to Sofia in a week in order to prepare the testimony for Long One's trial. Xena was also scheduled to appear as a witness in court, but the date of the trial was not yet known. He looked at her again, walked over to her and hugged her. He would enjoy every moment with her now.

Xena could see people looking at them. Some with envy, others with affection. Danny and she were a nice couple. She with honey blonde hair and blue eyes, he a brunette with deep dark eyes. Everyone could see how much they were in love. Apparently, they were considered newlyweds, young couples here were a usual sight. What she and Danny didn't realise was that the attraction between them was so visible. Every time they came out of the water, they attracted attention, not only were their beautiful athletic bodies impressive, but the way they cared for each other and the way they touched each other. It was hard to find a person in this small village who didn't know who they were. Even if they didn't want to be, they were part of the gossip here. The young girls longed to have a boyfriend like Danny and the men never missed Xena's daily surf. Watching her hair flying loose as she crested a wave was a joy to the eyes.

Xena didn't want all that attention. She longed for a little solitude with Danny, but finally resigned herself. There was no way to hide from people's eyes. They decided to spend more time in the house and go around the coast more. There weren't that many people there this time of year and when the weather was nice the views from some of the trails were amazing. Danny was already sorry he had to leave. There were many places he still wanted to visit with Xena. His English was good, and he often asked the locals about the history of the area.

At the beginning of the third week, as they walked along the coast, Xena and Danny heard a whimper. It came from a place they could not see, so the two of them descended a narrow, overgrown path and began to listen and look for the apparent frightened animal. The whimper grew louder, a dog barked. Danny took a side path, Xena decided to take another. At the end of her path, she saw a fluffy puppy. At first, she thought it was tangled in the bushes, but then she saw the rope. Someone had tied it tightly to a bush and dropped the dog down into the ocean. Xena shouted at Danny in horror. Who would want to do something like that with this cute little creature, she wondered. They both looked down the cliff, from what they saw the puppy was almost at water level, a tide was coming and soon the ocean would cover the dog. At first, Xena thought of cutting the rope, but Danny stopped her.

'If you do that, the dog will fall into the water and the waves will smash it into the rocks.'

'What do we do then?' she asked. If they pulled it up, the dog was in danger of being strangled.

'There is one way. I will go as close as possible, grab the bushes, and swing the rope to bring the puppy closer to me. That way I'll grab it by the fur and not the rope. It will hurt it, but we will get it out alive.'

'Let me do it. I'm lighter than you,' she said. 'If you have a belt, you can hold me, and I'll have a better chance of catching it right away.'

Danny agreed. He took his belt off his jeans and handed one end to Xena. She wrapped it around her right palm and began to descend toward the end of the cliff. As she approached, the rope rocked slightly. The puppy was frightened by this movement and began to howl piteously.

'Don't worry,' she assured him. 'We'll get you out.'

It looked at her with sad eyes and kept whimpering. Xena tried to get down a little further, but Danny stopped her.

'Try now, if you continue further down you may fall and then I will have to save both of you.'

She obeyed and tried to grab the rope as close to the dog as possible and rocked it slightly. The dog got scared and started writhing in fear. Xena couldn't catch it. The puppy was too scared and was trying to break free. She tried again, the animal was crying loudly as she grabbed the fur behind its ears, but remained calm, making no attempt to free itself. It clearly sensed that Xena was trying to save it. She pulled it out and put it on the ground. The poor puppy could barely stand on its feet. Its eyes were watery, and it was still looking scared and whimpering, as if expecting something bad was going to happen. Danny managed to untie the knot and release it permanently. Xena took the dog in her arms and tried to calm it down. She couldn't decide what breed it was. The puppy was the colour of a Golden Retriever, but its face didn't look like one.

'He's a boy,' Danny said.

'Yes, good boy,' Xena told the dog. 'We need to take him to the vet. I hope they didn't hurt him.'

Xena took the puppy and hugged him to her chest. She could feel his heart beating fast. She stroked him and tried to calm him, speaking softly to him as they descended the slope.

According to the vet, the dog was healthy, but he assumed that what happened to him would lead to problems in the future. Often such injuries led animals to fear of people and water.

'I'll write a report. I hope someone adopts him,' he said at last.

'I'll take him,' Xena said.

'I thought you were tourists?'

'Not exactly. I'm staying here, only my boyfriend is leaving.'

Danny looked at her questioningly but said nothing.

'Do you have experience with dogs?' the vet asked her.

'No, but I promise to train him and take good care of him,' Xena said. The vet asked her a few more questions, then said, 'Now you must tell me the name of this handsome boy.'

'Rocco,' Danny said.

'Rocco?' Xena looked at him in surprise, then laughed. She looked at the puppy and said, 'Let it be Rocco. It suits him, given where we found him.'

Rocco looked sad and was trembling with fear. The vet wrote down his name, gave him one of the mandatory vaccines and gave some advice to the young couple on how to raise the puppy, how to feed it, where they could enrol it in training and other important things.

Xena hugged Rocco tightly and led him to the house where they were staying. Danny and she made a temporary bed for him in the spare room, fed him, and let him sleep. Then they went and bought everything on the list the vet had made for them.

'Who would do such a thing to such a nice puppy?' Xena wondered.

'There are many bad people in this world, Xena. It's not like you haven't met such people.'

'You're right, but it's one thing to reach out to someone who can defend themself and quite another to tie up a puppy on purpose and let him struggle and watch the water hit him?'

'Believe me, if Rocco grows up big, I think he will know this man and will want to tear him apart. So, if they are local, sooner, or later you'll find out who it was.'

'Are you angry?' she asked gruffly.

'Why would I be angry with you?'

'I told the vet I would stay, and you would leave. I saw your gaze when I said that, but I thought that was your plan.'

'My plan is to return to you as often as possible and no, I'm not angry with you. Just when you said it out loud, I didn't like the idea of leaving you, but we both know I have no choice at the moment. As a matter of fact, I feel a little calmer now that I know you're going to have male company.'

Xena laughed.

'Yes, Rocco will keep me safe.'

'He'll grow up, you'll see,' he laughed. 'Then we'll both keep you safe.'

They went home and spent the whole evening working with Rocco. The dog had calmed down, even for a while playing with one of the toys, they had bought him.

'Well Rocco,' Xena told him. 'You're doing well for a three-month-old dog. Tomorrow, we will teach you to walk on a leash and we will take you for a walk to run ashore.'

Putting the collar on him was very difficult. Rocco was scared and kept pulling. The vet had told them that they might have a problem with this, as someone had already tied him up and his memories were not good. They had to walk him home first and eventually took him ashore to walk with them. Fortunately, Rocco was still small, not heavy and Danny and Xena could carry him.

After two days, they progressed to the stage of keeping him from trembling and letting him play more and more with the toys they had bought him. They often woke up at night and found him asleep at their feet, and in the mornings, he settled between them. His trust in them grew. Xena managed to talk to a dog trainer, who advised her at the moment to just establish a good relationship with the dog, to fully gain his trust and in a month or two, if he was better and able to perform several commands, to enrol him in training. Xena and Danny had their hands full looking after the dog, but they didn't mind taking care of the fluffy animal.

In the middle of the third week of their vacation, Xena and Danny decided to take Rocco to the beach restaurant for the first time. This was their favourite restaurant. Dogs were welcome, and they wanted to teach him to get used to standing still in such an environment. They sat at a table outside making Rocco sit between them. They had been to the restaurant a few times, and the owner, a tall blonde man with blue eyes named Brian, would often sit with them for a while and talk to them. As he headed to their table that evening with menus in hand, Rocco began growling to pull back in an attempt to escape. Xena and Danny reassured him, and he buried his nose in Xena's lap, but he kept making noises and shivering.

'Did you get a puppy?' Brian asked, sitting down next to them.

'Yes,' Danny said, 'we found him and adopted him.'

'Great. You have a souvenir from here.'

'Actually, he'll stay here,' Xena said, stroking Rocco's head. He looked at her with frightened eyes.

'He's scared,' she said. 'This is his first time out of the house since we found him.'

'Who will you leave it to?' Brian asked.

'I'll care for him. I'm thinking of staying here. Since we're on the subject, I'm looking for a job and accommodation. I can start early next week. I have worked as a saleswoman, a cleaner, and in bars and nightclubs. But, if necessary, I will work elsewhere. Do you think you could help me find something?'

'I'll ask,' Brian said. 'What kind of job are you looking for, Danny?'

'I'm not staying unfortunately. I will have to leave for a while.'
Brian looked at him in surprise.

'You look so happy and in love, everyone here envies you and you're breaking up,' the bar owner shook his head in disbelief. 'You are crazy people.'

'Only temporarily,' Danny said, but Brian didn't hear him. Someone called him, and he went to the kitchen.

Danny stared at Brian's back. It really was unbelievable that he had to leave. What Brian said saddened him. Rocco settled between the two of them again, looking at one or the other.

After eating, Danny took the dog in his arms and walked to the beach with Xena. Rocco watched the waves in fear, but the two of them calmed him down.

'I think Brian's right people envy us for looking happy together,' Danny said.

'That's right, but he's not right that we're going to break up, is he?'

'I won't leave you, Xena, you know that, but I have to go back to work, at least for a while.'

'I know and I know I put you in this situation. It was my decision to come and live here. It would be much easier just to stay with you in your apartment.'

'But you wouldn't be happy, and you know I'll rarely be at home because of my work. It doesn't matter if I come to see you here or there, but you will be happier and safe here. However, before I leave, I want to know where we will live and find you a job. Here the prices are quite high, I will leave you my savings to rent a nice house where we can live with Rocco.'

'We?' Xena laughed happily. 'I like it.'

She kissed Rocco on one protruding ear, then Danny. She had never felt so happy before. She started bouncing slightly as they walked along the beach. Danny thought she looked like a happy schoolgirl.

For two days, they travelled around looking for work for Xena and a house to live in. They found that there was no work, not only for Xena, but also for part of the local population. In general, most worked only during the tourist season, which was already beginning, and most hotels had already got staff. Also, again due to the tourist season, the houses for rent had become three times more expensive than a month ago. Xena began to despair. Danny and she began discussing the next day to go and look for a house farther from the ocean, as almost everyone had advised. In the evening, tired, they decided to take Rocco with them again and went to Brian's bar. The bar was open from ten in the morning until after midnight. There was often live music on the weekends. Food and drink were offered throughout the day and until late in the evening. One could meet both retirees there and young people who decided to spend their Friday night late with friends. Danny liked to go there at six o'clock, eat and drink quickly and then go home before the bar filled up later on. That night, there weren't many visitors, which was unusual, but the waiter told them they had an event later and people would probably come then.

As always, Brian sat down with them. Rocco buried his head in Xena's lap again, but this time he didn't growl, just hugged as much as he could. Xena hugged him and Danny stroked him to calm him down.

'Did you manage to find a job?' Brian asked.

'No, they have already hired people for the summer season everywhere.'

'You can work for me if you want. One of the girls is leaving at the end of next week. The pay is not the highest, but it will help you for a start.'

Xena looked at Danny and then laughed happily.

'Yes! Thank you. You will not regret it. I am used to working many hours and I have experience of parties.'

'Did you find a house?'

'No,' Danny said. 'They are busy for the season. We were advised to try in a more remote place because they are cheaper. We just can't afford the rent here.'

'Let me offer you something,' Brian said. 'I have a bungalow nearby. It's small, like for one person. I'll give it to Xena for a month, until she can find something more suitable.'

Xena looked at Danny again. It was a very strange offer, it was one thing to start working for Brian, but living in his bungalow bothered her. Danny said nothing.

'Think about it, take your time. If you want, check tomorrow and the next day for accommodation. If you find something, great. If not, my offer remains.'

Xena and Danny had dinner and left before the bar was full of people. They waved goodbye to Brian.

'Strange, don't you think?' said Xena. 'He offered me a job and accommodation.'

'You said they were very hospitable to you here the first time you came.'

'Yes, but I don't know.'

'As far as I know, he won't give us the bungalow for no money. We will pay rent.'

'You're right. I'm just suspicious, you know what I've been through.'

'Let's keep looking for a house tomorrow and the day after tomorrow. If we don't find one, we'll have to take advantage of Brian's offer. I will ask an acquaintance from London to check on Brian, to put our minds at rest.'

'All right,' Xena said. 'It's just weird that everything works out like a magic wand. You know, it's not usually that easy for me. Luckily, I met you.'

She stopped and kissed him. Rocco rebelled as the two unwittingly hugged him.

Danny and Xena didn't sleep all night. They only had three nights left together. They made love, talked to each other, dreamed of a day when there would be no need to separate.

'We have never discussed this before, but do you want to have children?' Xena asked him.

'I thought it was impossible in our case,' Danny told her.

'Not now, but later,' she whispered.

Danny tightened his grip on her. In the dawn light, Xena saw the change in the colour of his eyes.

'What?' she asked. 'What did I say?'

'Nothing,' he said, but she sensed something.

'Danny?'

Their eyes met.

'Dary didn't even tell you, did she?' he said sadly.

'What did Dary not tell me?' she asked insistently.

'You know, I just don't like telling you bad news,' he said and hugged her.

She pulled away from his embrace and looked at him intently again. He sighed heavily and told her.

'Dary promised me to talk to you before we left. She didn't tell you in the hospital because she didn't have the courage.'

'Danny, just tell me. Please.'

'There were complications when you lost your baby. The chances of having a child are very small.'

A groan escaped Xena. She lay on his chest, then stood up and said, 'So, there's still a chance, albeit a small one.'

Danny sighed again. He hated it, he hated telling her things that hurt her.

'When we were looking for you, we took your medical card because the doctor didn't want to talk to us. The doctor who reviewed your medical records was adamant that the blows that Long One had inflicted on you had caused internal injuries and...'

'Don't,' Xena interrupted. She got out of bed. Then she came back to him and hugged him.

'I am very sorry,' he whispered to her, holding her close. 'I thought you knew.'

Xena nodded and despite her best efforts not to cry the tears welled up. Her grief came from a deep place, passed through her tight throat, and turned into hiccups and sobs. Rocco heard her cry and began to whimper from the other room. Danny released Xena for a moment, took the little puppy and laid him on the bed with them. Rocco saw the tears and began to lick them. Danny stroked her hair and tried to calm her.

'I told you we'd both take care of you,' he reminded her, kissing her. 'I know it's hard for you and I want to kill the bastard who did this to you.'

Rocco continued to clean her face, forcing Xena to get up and push him away. This sweet creature and this wonderful man were giving her something she didn't think she could have again. Love. She stood up, kissed them both and with sadness in her voice and eyes told Danny that it was not his fault. Xena knew what she was up to now and she didn't want to give in to her grief at that moment. She would do it when Danny left.

Xena and Danny spent two days in search of housing but didn't find anything. In the end, they agreed that they should accept Brian's offer. One day before Danny left, he and Xena went to the bar, took the key to the bungalow, and carried their luggage there. The bungalow was small, with a small kitchen, a small bedroom, a bathroom, and a corridor. It was enough for her and Rocco at first. Brian told them they could pay the rent later, but Danny insisted and paid. He didn't want to leave Xena with pending rent. He didn't want to leave her at all, he wanted to take her with him, as did Rocco. He knew, however, that this could not happen, at least for the time being. His intuition told him something was wrong, but he couldn't figure out what.

They only had one night left before Danny left so they decided to get sandwiches and not go out. They wanted to spend every remaining minute alone, they made love, played with Rocco, and talked until morning. They hugged until the sun rose.

'I don't want to go,' Danny told her.

'I know and I don't want you to leave.'

'I'll be back,' Danny said, not only to her but to the dog. 'I'll be back as soon as possible.'

'Rocco and I will be waiting for you,' Xena said and cried. Danny hugged her and held her like that for a while. He had never felt that way before. He couldn't tear himself away from her. He was afraid that something bad would happen to her while he was gone. He squeezed her hard and it hurt a little. She moaned, raised her head, and kissed him.

'I have to go,' Danny said in a husky voice. Xena slowly released herself from his embrace and nodded. It had never been so difficult for her to say goodbye to someone. She feared that he would not return and that she would see him for the last time. Her voice trembled as she said, 'Have a nice trip.'

'I'll call you when I get to London.'

'All right. I'll wait.'

She was standing in the doorway. Tears streamed down her cheek. Rocco stood beside her and whimpered.

'I'll be back, I promise,' Danny said in an emotional voice. He bent down, kissed Xena, then he took Rocco in his arms, kissed him on the head and whispered, 'Protect her.'

Rocco raised his head and began to lick his face. Danny set him carefully on the ground, kissed Xena again and left. He waved goodbye from the taxi several times.

When the car disappeared from the road, Xena closed the front door and went into the bathroom to take a shower. She left the bathroom door open for Rocco to see her; his bed was placed directly opposite the door. The dog was curled up and looking at her sadly. Xena took a shower, left her phone nearby in case Danny called her, undressed, and went under the warm streams of water. The separation was hard for her, tears were flowing, a heavy loud cry came from her chest. She didn't try to stop the tears, instead she sat on the floor in the shower and cried with all her heart and soul.

For two days, Xena barely left the bungalow. She took Rocco for a walk in the nearby forest and avoided people. She didn't want anyone to see her suffer. The absence of the man she loved so much caused her physical and mental pain. She took his clothes, squeezed them in her hands and inhaled his scent. Xena had never imagined that she could feel so lonely and miss someone that much. She often hugged Rocco and just cried. She kept her phone on all the time, often clinging to it as her hand sweated. She listened, hoping to hear Danny's footsteps and voice. Xena hoped he would surprise her and come back to her. Their separation affected her mentally. She couldn't sleep, she couldn't eat, and she couldn't think of anything else. Xena thought only of him and how much she missed him. She knew it wasn't easy for him either. She had felt it in his voice; had felt his emotion on the other end of the phone line. He missed her too; she was sure of that.

Danny had called her from London, then called her when he got back to his apartment. It had been difficult for both of them to talk, but they had spent almost an hour on the phone, sometime just in quiet silence, as did the people who missed each other. It was as if they were next to each other, but they couldn't touch. A painful separation engulfed both of them.

Danny tried to calm her down, to make her think about her new job and little Rocco, who needed longer walks. He made her promise to get out of the bungalow and go for a long walk on the beach. She agreed with him. She had to start somewhere.

On the third day, Xena took Rocco for a walk and decided to run with him to the shore. She hoped this would cheer her up, but at the sight of several couples in love, her heart sank, and she headed to the bar to talk to Brian about when she could start work. He was out and the waiter and bartender didn't know that a new person was working with them or that anyone had left work. Brian probably hadn't told them yet, Xena thought. She stopped at a nearby store to buy something for lunch, then went back to the bungalow.

Danny also had a tough time. Not only did he miss Xena, but he also worried about her. She hadn't sounded good on the phone, and his sense that something was wrong kept worrying him. He had been trying to find information about Brian for several days, but so far there was none.

Danny hoped to be able to return to Xena soon and find a house in the long run. The one-month period bothered him, he didn't want her and the dog to be out on the streets one day and not be there to help them. He was doing his best to get his paperwork done and get back to her quickly, but he hadn't told her yet that it could be sooner than she thought.

Xena was busy training Rocco to get up and sit under command. She gave him a treat, encouraged him with words and in an hour, he was making great progress. She fed him and decided that was enough for the day and that it was time for both of them to rest.

It was past four when Danny called her. She was just getting dressed after a short shower in the bathroom.

'How are you?' he asked her. There was a sound of concern in his voice.

'Good. How are you?'

'Xena, I have something very important to tell you,' Danny said, his tone was very serious this time.

Xena was worried and wondered what he meant, but just then the doorbell rang.

'Just a second, I'll be right back. It's probably the courier,' she told Danny. She set the phone on the bathroom cabinet and opened the front door.

As soon as the door opened, Brian and two other men pushed her toward the bedroom. Xena tried to pull away but failed. Rocco began to whimper and bark, and Xena cried for help. One of the men put his hand over her mouth and knocked her onto the bed. The other squeezed her hands and tied them high. Brian kicked the dog and locked him in the bathroom. Rocco continued to whimper but stopped barking. Xena got angry and tried with inhuman strength to free herself to try to help him. However, the three men pinned her.

'Your boyfriend is gone and since we knew you would be lonely and sad, we decided to come and keep you company,' Brian told her.

Xena kept trying to free herself, but with her hands tied and pressed by three men, her chances were low.

'We watched you two have fun in bed that night. You're good. But you Xena, you are better, you are flexible. We said to ourselves, we can also take advantage,' added one of the men. Xena had seen him often at the bar, as had Brian's friend. Her horror grew, she knew these three were dangerous. Her only reassurance came in the hope that Danny had heard them attack her and would call for help. She just had to hold on.

Brian played a video of her and Danny in bed.

'Incredible sex. If you want us to leave you alive, you will reward us one by one,' he told her, looking her straight in the eyes.

'If you shout, I'll kill the dog first, then I'll make you disappear.'

Xena tried to resist, but two of the men were taking her clothes off. In order not to untie her hands, they tore the t-shirt she was wearing.

'She even took a bath for us. She obviously knew we were coming,' one man laughed wickedly.

'But I want to start with the extra,' Brian said. 'I love oral love.'

He unbuttoned his jeans, unzipped, and gestured to his friend to remove his hand from her mouth.

'If you call, I'll kill you,' he warned her. He pulled out his cock and aimed it at her mouth. Xena turned away in disgust.

'Work, bitch. I promised you a good job and a home. Now it's time to earn them,' he hissed. She turned and bit him hard.

Brian screamed and this made his friends let her go. She walked to the door, but one of them recovered and grabbed her. He laid her on the bed and started hitting her. Xena's face flushed with blood.

'Bitch,' Brian shouted and jumped, screaming loudly from the pain in his groin. His face was flushed, and tears welled up in his eyes.

His friend called a doctor on the phone and made him come urgently. Xena thought the doctor might help her, but Brian came out and according to his friends, helped drag him into the bungalow next door. The man who stayed with her continued to hit her. Eventually, Xena fainted.

When she regained consciousness, she found that she couldn't move. Her head ached and she felt her mouth stick with tape. She wanted to remove it, but she couldn't move her hand. Her eyes were swollen, she tried to open them, but she couldn't. Severe pain pierced her and prevented her from seeing. Something tickled her ear, she tried to raise her hand again, but something pinned her hand. With great effort she opened her right eye and was horrified by what she saw. She was on the shore of the ocean, she could hear the waves, it was dark, and she could see only a faint glimmer of them. Her chin rested on the sand. With terror, she realised that she had been buried in the sand up to her neck. Only her head was visible. Xena felt sick. She tried to calm down, but panic gripped her more and more with every second. Now she knew who had tied Rocco to the rocks. The dirty bastards wanted to do the same to her. The tide would come to her and drown her slowly and painfully. The thought hurt her even more. This quickened her breathing and caused severe pain in her chest. Her body was buried, not even one of her fingers could move. Panic gripped her again. She had been sentenced to a slow and painful death. This time hatred flooded her body. Her headache intensified and she tried again to calm down and try to better assess the situation. Xena couldn't move her head, so she couldn't tell which beach it was on, she only knew it wasn't too late because she could see lights from the houses across the way.

She figured the waves were still far away, so she had between half an hour and an hour to try to get out. She made another effort to move her body, but it felt as if it had been walled up. She couldn't call for help, the patch on her mouth was thick, she couldn't remove it. Little by little, insects began to creep up her head. Probably some of them were the little spiders they sometimes saw on the beach. She could feel something moving in her ears and others moving in her face and eyes. She tried to ignore it, directing her thoughts to Danny. Where was he? Didn't he realise she was in danger? And what did these freaks do with Rocco?

Her eyes watered. It wasn't fair, everything was just starting to work out. The life, what the life didn't offer her? Life was both good and bad—a dose of happiness and a dose of luck and just when she was in love, healthy and happy, the same life was trying to take it away from her.

She wasn't born to live a happy life, she now understood, here in the sand. Xena heard the waves approaching. She even began to feel more moisture around her. She tried to calm down, but the horror of what was coming stunned her, darkened her eyes and she lost consciousness again.

When she came round, ants and spiders began to take over her head, but she tried to ignore them and remain numb, so she wouldn't feel their movement. The waves were approaching, only two steps away, when a dog's bark broke the silence.

The dog came to the young woman's head and began to whimper and bark. A man stood beside the dog, pointed his phone down and when he saw Xena's head, he called out for help.

The dog and the man began digging frantically in the sand in an attempt to free her. Two other dogs arrived and began digging a hole, sometimes injuring Xena's skin. She recovered, tried to open her eyes, but couldn't. Someone had removed the sticker from her mouth, and she moaned.

'Thank God you're alive!' a familiar voice said.

'Gal?' Xena whispered hard.

'I told you I'd come just when you needed me the most,' Gal said as he tried to dig her out. 'Danny called me last night and sent me here. He didn't want to leave you alone. Something bothered him and he was right. He tried to warn you, but just when he wanted to tell you about Brian, you left your phone and walked to the door. It was his idea to let Rocco lead me to you.'

Gal spoke quickly, while at the same time trying to scoop up as much sand as possible and free her. Some police officers had come to the rescue, but the waves were coming faster than expected and water was gathering around Xena's body. More people came to help and made a dyke to divert the water.

Xena recognised Rocco's whimper. She tried to smile, then something pierced her and slowly, very slowly, she sank into darkness.

'Xena! Xena!' Gal tried to bring her back to her senses, but Xena remained motionless. She could hear Gal's voice, but the darkness enveloped her more and more, until she finally heard and felt nothing. The abyss dragged her, and she sank deep into the darkness.

Facebook page @Hristina Bloomfield Author

Also by Hristina Bloomfield

Becky

Her life will pass through your fingers as you read this book.

Sixteen-year-old Becky is raped and left lying with multiple stab wounds on the Cornwall coast. Instead of supporting and helping her in this difficult time, her parents send her to London, where her cousin Arnie promises to take care of her. Arnie and his roommates Paul and Alex help her recover. When the police fail to find the perpetrators, the three men hire private detectives to help with the investigation. Becky accepts their help and in time, she and the lawyer Alex become very good friends. The difficulties they have to go through even bring them closer together. Becky and Alex fight both against her abusers and against her family, which keeps causing her trouble. After many vicissitudes, Becky finally finds justice. But fate does not let her enjoy her new life. She experiences loss after loss.

Becky's story has pain and betrayal as well as friendship, hope, and very strong love, the loss of which will be difficult for her.

Kurt

Fifty-six-year-old rock star Kurt and his rock band set up to create their new album in Cornwall. They are joined by the lyricist Leah, who agrees to help them with the lyrics for the new songs. Everything is going well until one night one of the band's roadie and Leah's taxi driver are killed. Clues led to two different killers. One wants to kill Kurt and the other Leah. Then both are subsequently shot by a sniper.

The investigation was unsuccessful, and the police inspectors send Leah far away and use Kurt to get the killers to show up.

However, new revelations about Leah's identity confuse the musician. Kurt's life will turn in an unexpected direction for him, and new and new revelations will make Kurt realize that he has unwittingly intervened in something from which he will hardly be able to escape.

The Story of a Thief

Tony was born into a family of thieves. His life seems predestined, until his girlfriend Eva disappears suddenly. For several years he put all his skills into finding her, even working in the police, but there is no sign of his girlfriend. In several of the investigations he leads, Tony works with a psychic who uses Tarot cards. He is so impressed by her gift so he decides to tell her his story with the hope that she will help him to find Eva. However, it turns out that Isabella's life is no less complicated than his. The two have a lot in common and this creates tension and romance in their relationship. In the course of their investigation, Tony and Isabella discover that nothing is as it seems.

Manufactured by Amazon.ca
Bolton, ON

45437123R00144